ANNIE'S ATTIC MYSTERIES

Medals
in the Attic

Cathy Elliott

AnniesMysteries.com

Published in Association with
Stenhouse & Associates, Ridgefield, Connecticut

Jacket & Book Design by
Lookout Design, Inc., Minneapolis, Minnesota

Library of Congress-in-Publication Data
Medals in the Attic / by Cathy Elliott
p. cm.
ISBN: 978-1-59635-296-4
I. Title
                    2009908722

10 11 12 13 14 | Printed in China | 10 9 8 7 6 5 4 3 2

AnniesMysteries.com
800-282-6643

～ 1 ～

"Maybe this is the one!" Annie Dawson tore open another dust-covered cardboard box and pulled out the contents. More table linens. Disappointed, she refolded the cross-stitched napkins and arranged them on the matching tablecloth. Lovely, but not what she wanted. "It's just got to be in one of these boxes. Gram told me she packed it away."

"When was that? Thirty years ago?" Alice MacFarlane, Annie's childhood friend, asked as she sorted through boxes nearby. "After more than an hour of searching, be happy we found that toy china set—the moss rose pattern. And by accident, I remind you." She separated the container with the tiny tea service from the others and placed it atop an old bird's-eye maple dressing table.

"Believe me, I'm thrilled to find them. It's like a miracle. I mean, look at this clutter." Annie waved her arms to highlight the attic's jumble of furniture, clothing, and stacks of boxes with who-knows-what inside.

Annie was sure that one of them contained a small doll's afghan she'd crocheted as a young girl under her grandmother's guidance. She pictured Gram's crochet hook darting in and out as she demonstrated the techniques. At the time, Annie couldn't know what a rarity it was for her grandmother to teach the technique.

Gram's instructional time was usually reserved for cross-stitching. But because of Annie's strong interest in crochet, Betsy had put aside her own preference to teach the child her chosen craft. And crocheting had become Annie's lifelong creative pursuit.

"Let's keep looking. I'd love to find that afghan. It could be a perfect gift for my granddaughter."

"Well, good luck with that," Alice said, eyeing the mess. "Why don't you give her the dishes, instead?"

Not a bad idea. Annie considered it. "Joanna's only five years old. That's a bit young for china. She can't break the afghan."

"Okay, makes sense. So what wonderful memento will you find for the other twin? Got an old set of Grandpa Holden's camping gear hidden around here for John?"

Annie stood up and stretched, getting the kinks out of her legs. "Maybe there's something over there he'd like," she said, gesturing toward a different stack of boxes. "We could dive into those."

"No diving in the attic. I'm sure Betsy used to say that. Besides, weren't we looking for an *object d'art* to donate to the auction next weekend?"

"True. I guess I *have* gotten a little distracted. It's just so hard to give any of Gram's things away. Like I'm tossing aside an important piece of her life somehow." Annie frowned and bit her lip.

"That's just natural, Annie. After all, Betsy passed away only a short time ago. You want to hold on to her possessions—to what reminds you of her. Maybe you could donate something less personal?"

Alice pointed across the room, beyond some sheeted shapes that hinted at high-back chairs. "Over near that old washstand. Take a look in that trunk. It's bursting with books and some really nice prints. I put one on the top for you to check out. It's a signed Wallace Nutting. Might bring in a good price. It's for charity, you know."

"I know," Annie agreed. "I guess I can donate something Gram collected as long as I don't have to give up anything she actually made. Too close to the heart."

"If you add the old print to the gorgeous afghan you're crocheting, it's a very generous donation. I still don't know what I'm going to give." Alice restacked some wayward boxes and then paused. "Much as I hate to miss out on any more amazing archaeological finds, my friend, I gotta go. Even the storm outside does not daunt when duty calls. I have a Divine Décor party to host later." She brushed away dust that had adhered to her T-shirt like Christmas tree flocking. "What am I? A lint magnet?"

"No. You're a friend magnet." Annie said, removing a cobweb from Alice's auburn hair. "This was fun. Thanks for your help."

"Any time. It makes me remember all our tea parties on that mismatched china. You never let me use the moss rose set. Hmm. I wonder why."

"Maybe because you were a bit clumsy, as I recall. I kept the little dishes for my dollies. Sorry." Annie looked apologetic. "But we did have fun dressing up, remember?"

"Weren't we just too glamorous wearing your grandmother's old clothes? What a wealth of memories is in this attic."

"Memories I wouldn't trade for anything," Annie said. "And the good news is, we still have more to make."

"I'm so happy you came back to us, Annie. Except for the reason. . .Betsy's passing. But don't forget, tomorrow is Tuesday, Hook and Needle Club time. I'll be by to pick you up."

"Come early for tea," Annie said. "And crumpets. If I can figure out what a crumpet is. . ."

"Let the crumpet sound!" Alice said, grinning. She picked her way through the "aisles" and headed down the stairs. "Remember. Look in the trunk." She waved and closed the attic door.

Annie shook her head and smiled. She hadn't realized when she returned to Stony Point, Maine, to settle her grandmother's affairs that she would inherit more than the old Victorian house, Grey Gables. She would also reunite with her childhood friend. Annie had been given much in a very short time. Her heart was full of gratitude. And sadness.

Sighing, she navigated over to the trunk, touching familiar objects fondly along the way. Each piece had a story, she imagined. What secrets did they hold?

A gray shadow flitted across the path, making Annie jump. But it was only Boots—Gram's sometimes finicky feline—inherited with the old house. She must have slipped in when Alice opened the attic door. No matter. A little cat company was always welcome.

Seated on a squat stool, Annie gazed at the old hand-tinted photo she had just liberated from the trunk. It had lain on top of the pile of pictures stacked inside. Framed simply, it depicted a genteel lady in nineteenth-century dress, gloved hand outstretched to help down a friend from a stagecoach. Or perhaps she was about to climb on board. And embark on a marvelous journey.

Annie knew a bit about journeys. It hadn't been that long since she, too, bravely set out from her home in Brookfield, Texas, for unexpected adventure right here in Stony Point. She'd never dreamed . . .

A loud crash startled her and she lost her grip on the picture. Fumbling at the frame, Annie caught it before it clattered to the floor. She clutched it to her chest, heart pounding, and whirled around to find only Boots. The cat sat on the tiny window seat, frantically grooming her cobweb-covered coat. A fallen Victorian lamp with beaded fringe splayed about must have caused the racket. But Boots didn't know anything about that. No, ma'am.

"Boots! Are you okay?" Annie returned the picture to the trunk and picked her way across the chaos. There wasn't much room between the boxes and booty stacked in every attic opening, but she managed to reach Boots without mishap and scooped her up. Scratching behind the feline's ears and finger combing dust from the soft gray fur, Annie asked, "Did that nasty lamp try to get you?"

Enclosing the cat in one more comforting snuggle, Annie deposited the four white paws on the floor and gave Boots a little push. "Off with you, troublemaker." The cat scooted toward the stairs.

"I'll be glad to clean this up for you, Miss Boots," Annie called after her. She hadn't planned to spend any time in the attic today, much less straightening up after her pesky pet. But the stormy afternoon had changed her hopes of a trek into Stony Point for more merino wool. And maybe, if she was lucky, a bit of conversation at A Stitch in Time, the local yarn shop. The wool would have to wait.

Looking for a project, the two friends had decided to search for something among Gram's attic treasures for Annie to donate for the annual community center auction.

And now, thankfully, the print proved promising. In mint condition, it should fetch a good price for the building fund. Even signed by the photographer. A little sparkling up would make it irresistible to the most reluctant bidder.

Annie righted the lamp and carried it to a safe corner, the beaded fringe tinkling like tiny chimes. There didn't appear to be any damage to the fine old piece. A rolled-up Persian rug propped nearby must have cushioned its fall. Annie examined the carpet, running her hand along its back. The exposed inside edge showed a bright and colorful pattern, but the outside looked more like a cat scratching post. Annie heaved away the heavy roll to make it less accessible to somebody's claws and noticed a small cardboard box buried beneath.

Intrigued, she let the rug fall to the side and sat cross-legged on the floor. Lifting the box, she spotted a scrawl on the sides: "Keep." Annie caught her breath. This must be something special of Gram's. Wouldn't it be great if it were the little doll afghan? Blowing away bits of dust and trying not to sneeze, she pried open the top.

She pulled away a layer of crushed newspaper to reveal some cotton cloth covering a rectangular shape. Not the afghan, but interesting anyway. Annie lifted it from the cozy nest and carefully pulled off the cloth. Underneath the wrinkled cotton, one of Gram's cross-stitched tea towels, rested a carved wooden case. The glass top exposed what appeared to be two medals. Military medals. Awed, she stared at them. How stirring.

And how strange.

Grandpa Holden's World War II medals were displayed in the living room in a shadow box, along with other of his wartime memorabilia. So whose medals were these?

Annie contemplated the case. They must belong to Grandpa. Who else? If they were indeed his medals, why were they packed away? Why not celebrate them with the family?

"Maybe it's a secret!" Her voice cut through the patter of rain on the roof. But why would Gram and Grandpa keep such spectacular honors a secret?

That was a good question. With no instant answer.

The medals were mounted on a backdrop of black, velvety fabric. One, a heart-shaped medal, hung from purple ribbon. In the center of the heart, a likeness of George Washington silhouetted in gold. Annie knew what this medal represented. It wasn't awarded for frostbite or the flu but given only to servicemen wounded in battle. Or killed.

The Purple Heart.

Grandpa often said how much he appreciated his guardian angel. He'd gotten through the war years without a scrape. So it couldn't be his, could it?

She didn't recognize the other medal. A gold five-pointed star, it reminded her a little of the Stony Point sheriff's badge—attached to a blue ribbon by a clasp imprinted with thirteen stars. Very handsome. It looked important. But again, why wasn't it on display with the others?

Annie repacked the box, securing the case inside, and stood, glad to end the session on these old wooden planks. She grabbed the box containing her childhood tea service and set the medals on top. Remembering the Nutting print, she removed it from the trunk and let the lid close with a clank. Then, cradling the box under one arm and clutching the print with her empty hand, she took one last look at the cluttered room.

It being filled with years of memorabilia and memories, she felt closer to Gram in this room than any other. Revisiting tea parties and other enchanting attic adventures with Alice today helped bring her old, unburdened self closer, too. Before all the loss. Within these walls were precious things long forgotten—enduring evidence of lives richly lived.

And secrets.

The baffling box of medals proved that.

Looks like you've given me another mystery to solve, Gram.

~ 2 ~

Boots waited at the top of the stairs, tail twitching. Then she sauntered over and rubbed against Annie's jeans, the scolding apparently forgotten. With both arms full of rescued treasure, her mistress couldn't attend to Boots. Undeterred, the assertive cat threaded through and around Annie's legs as she took the steps, one by one.

"Really, Boots. It's impossible to walk down this staircase with you tripping me up." She shoved the cat aside with one foot, a gentle slide toward the wall. Acting insulted, Boots avoided eye contact and pondered her paw before loping down to the next floor.

Unable to grasp the stair rail, Annie leaned against it, glad it seemed sturdy. She hadn't noticed it loose before. There really wasn't much repair required indoors at Grey Gables. But she'd had no idea the old Victorian would need any sprucing up at all when she'd inherited it from Gram only months before. Thank heaven for wonderful Wally Carson, her handyman. The outside already showed the fine results of his skills.

When Annie's heel caught on the next step, she reached for the railing, whacking the picture frame against the wood. *Great.* Now she had probably broken the wonderful old swirly glass that had lasted for how long? Eighty years, give or take a decade. If she replaced it, the picture wouldn't be mint anymore. It would have replacement glass. And the value would plummet. For it to earn any real money for the auction, someone would have to bid just out of kindness.

I guess that someone would be me.

Two trips might have been a good idea.

Arriving at the landing, Annie turned to see her reflection in an antique mirror hung above a petite chair. Blond hair, recently trimmed to chin length and dulled by the dust picked up in the attic. How did that happen? She hadn't mopped the floor with her head. Yet it looked more cobwebby than Alice's. Even Annie's sparkles, what the grandchildren called her ever-encroaching gray hair, were lackluster.

Thinking of Joanna and John's creativity gave her heart a twinge. In the mirror, her green eyes softened. How she wished they were here at Grey Gables. This very minute. Good heavens, they could help carry these hefty boxes down the stairs. Or at least summon help if she stumbled.

It then occurred to Annie that if she fell and broke a leg, or worse, both legs, she would be trapped between floors. Alone. With only Boots to the rescue. Maybe she could drag herself to the bedroom and pull the phone to the floor. It painted a desperate picture. Had Gram worried about this very thing? That may be why the attic was so unkempt. In her final years, had the risk of taking the extra flight of stairs been too great?

A familiar guilt incriminated Annie, one felt often since coming to Grey Gables. Why hadn't she come sooner? While Gram was still alive? Since her husband's death last year, Annie hadn't had the heart to do anything but miss Wayne. Their home together in Brookfield, those wonderful times raising LeeAnn, the years working with him at their Chevy dealership. She still missed him every day. Such a deep, deep loss. Built on her mother's passing five years before, followed by her father's two years later. And now Gram was gone. Still so many unspoken words left to say to all these dear ones.

Annie shook her head. Regret too often her companion, she resolved to think on the sweetness of her memories and continued down the stairs.

Once in the living room, she released the boxes to the safety of the sofa and scrutinized the print. The glass wasn't cracked, nor the frame. The scene captured her anew, feeling a kinship with the woman in the picture.

Annie nestled into the sofa and bumped against the medals. Putting the print aside, she reopened the box. This time, she smoothed out crumpled newspapers, noting they were pages from the *The Point*, dated from the 1950s. Would she find a clue in the columns, leading her to the owner of the medals? She didn't know but resolved to save them to devour later, if only for history's sake. It would be fun to see what the Stony Point neighbors were doing during that decade. Or rather, what their parents had been doing.

A perfect rainy-day activity.

The carvings on the case were simple but elegant, with a patriotic theme. Combined with the medals, the effect was much like experiencing the Fourth of July. Someone gave a great deal for freedom. Maybe someone gave all.

Annie inspected the woodwork, wondering if Grandpa was the artisan. She remembered evenings sitting with her grandparents on the front porch, he whittling figurines and she stitching up another masterpiece. Grandpa possessed the ability to carve the bunting-like edge, starred corners, and the American eagle that adorned the glass lid. To Annie, the wood looked like mahogany. Soft enough for carving, Grandpa said, though he liked pine better.

She set the case on the coffee table and returned to the cardboard box. Had she missed anything? She tossed the remaining crushed newspapers onto the floor where Boots began batting them about.

Her pulse quickened. There was something. At the bottom lay a sealed, white envelope labeled "Save. 1942." Annie ripped open the flap, felt inside, and withdrew three sepia-toned photos of a man in naval uniform. In one shot, he held the hand of a woman; the others showed him alone on a pier. Was that taken at the harbor? Or in a foreign port? And who were they?

The woman resembled a young Betsy Holden in form, but the faded and grainy picture made it hard to tell. Besides, the woman's body faced the sailor, and she wore a hat. Annie squinted at the shot. Neither person looked familiar.

Nice hat, though.

Annie flipped over the pictures, one by one. Nothing. No writing at all. Still, because they were packed with the carved case, perhaps they held a clue to the ownership of the medals. Except for the photographs, the cardboard box was empty.

Standing and facing the window, Annie could see the storm had no intention of slacking off. The view from the Grey Gables front porch usually proved picture postcard-worthy. A grassy lawn gently sloped down to the road, and far beyond one could see the ocean. But today the rain fell in torrents and wind bent the bushes with powerful gusts. Annie's attitude churned along with the Atlantic.

"I thought today was supposed to be filled with scattered showers," she said, hands on hips. "So scatter!" She followed the order with a foot stomp.

It didn't work.

Annie stared outside with longing. On a nice day, she might take a leisurely walk, listen to the gulls overhead, and inhale the salty air. Now, trapped inside, she felt restless and unsettled. Maybe a little cabin-bound.

She glanced at the floral-print sofa and the other worn but well-appointed furnishings in the living room. The adjacent formal dining room with its graceful table and china cabinet extended the charm. And finally, Annie eyed the entry and the framed country scene hanging there. Her favorite of all Gram's handiwork. The first original Betsy Holden cross-stitch.

Smiling, she whispered, "Thanks, Gram. For everything."

Annie had a sudden urge to call her daughter in Texas and hear that sweet drawl in her ear again. Perhaps grab a little grandma-time with the twins. She punched in the number.

"Sorry, Mom. I dropped the kids off at vacation Bible school over an hour ago."

LeeAnn, probably enjoying a couple of rare hours of leisure, didn't sound all that sorry to Annie, who had forgotten about their plans. "Any chance they'll be home soon? Their grandma is missing them."

"They miss you, too, Mom. And so do I. Any chance you'll be home soon?"

Did Annie hear a smile in her daughter's voice or not? This was an argument better left unargued.

Changing the subject, Annie asked, "LeeAnn, did Great-Grandpa ever mention anything to you about military medals? Like maybe a Purple Heart? Or another important medal?"

"I don't think so. Not that I recall, anyway. He served in World War II, right?"

"Right." Annie nodded and ambled toward the kitchen. "There are some medals, along with ribbons, displayed in a shadow box here at Grey Gables."

"There you are, then," LeeAnn said. "I don't really get what you are asking."

Annie chose a chair and sat at the old farm table. This might take a while to explain.

"While I was in the attic searching for something to donate to the community center auction, I found a couple of other medals. They're beautiful. But I can't figure out if they belong to Grandpa or not."

"Well, of course they do. Who else?" LeeAnn asked. "By the way, Mom, I don't think it's such a good idea for you to be rifling around in that attic."

"Why not?"

"Who knows what's up there? If you found World War

ll medals, maybe you'll find weapons, too. What if there's an old grenade? Or something worse?" LeeAnn asked, her tone turning anxious. "Now that I think about it, I don't know if I can sleep thinking about you prowling around up there."

"LeeAnn!" Annie said. "Don't be silly. Do you really think Grandpa Holden would leave anything dangerous up in the attic when he knew his wife liked to putter among her stored treasures?"

There was a silence on the other end of the line. Finally LeeAnn gave in. "No. I guess he wouldn't. But even if there are no weapons hidden in there, it's so full of junk you could break your leg just walking from one side of the attic to the other. Did you ever think of that?"

Annie didn't want to tell her daughter she had the same thought coming down the stairs today. If she said anything, a plane ticket would be waiting to take her home by noon tomorrow. And Annie wasn't ready to go. Yet.

But she could feel LeeAnn's concern between the lines. "Don't worry, honey," Annie said, trying to inject a lighter tone. "This is Stony Point. There's no safer place on earth. Nothing's going to happen to me here."

She hoped her assurances had soothed her daughter's distress. Though, for Annie, discussing the medals had only served to peak her interest in their ownership. There had to be an explanation out there.

And she planned to stay in Stony Point long enough to find it.

~ 3 ~

*T*he next morning Annie took an early walk down to the road, enjoying the sun's rays breaking through cumulus clouds. The storm had moved on. The view of the ocean was magnificent. Gulls dotted the seascape, bobbing like tiny sailboats. In the distance, a few pleasure skiffs cut across the channel, off to catch the-one-that-got-away last year. Tourists, no doubt. The real fishing began long before the sun rose.

The walk had worked its magic and the fresh salt air invigorated Annie's troubled psyche. Last night she couldn't stop brooding about the medals and those old pictures found in the attic. She spent several hours trying to complete her current crochet project—a lovely afghan in vibrant colors of wool—but didn't get far. She kept stopping to wonder about the medals.

Annie continued to ponder them now as she lingered in her yard, staring toward the sea, formulating a first step in her investigation. If one could call it that. Her inquiry? That sounded better. Less like a private eye without a license.

Or a clue, for that matter.

"Hey, Annie!" A voice interrupted. "It's cold out here." Alice stood beside her car, pushing her sweater-jacket down over her fists. "Stop that wool-gathering and let's go inside."

Alice lived nearby in an old carriage house and often trekked over on foot for a visit. Today she had driven her flashy Ford Mustang into the Grey Gables driveway, apparently without being noticed by her otherwise-absorbed friend.

Annie hurried toward the porch and opened the door for Alice. They chatted down the hall to the kitchen. Boots followed, probably hoping for a snack. Well acquainted with Alice, who had cared for the cat after Annie's grandmother Betsy had passed away, Boots wasn't picky about who served the snack. As long as it was served.

"Excuse the mess, Alice. Wally started the kitchen remodel a few days ago. The old wallpaper is out. The backsplash is gone. Ready for a new look." Annie gave the kitchen a critical review.

"Let me know if you need my help. I'm pretty handy with a brush. And of course I am privy to the entire Divine Décor catalog at 30 percent off retail. Even some things you can't buy anymore."

"Thanks, I appreciate that, Alice. Really."

"Glad to be of assistance."

"Wait until you hear what I found in the attic after you left." Annie dropped a sideways glance as she filled the kettle with cold water from the tap.

"You're kidding. You found the doll afghan?"

"No, not the afghan. I forgot all about that. But, now that you bring up the subject, I do want to locate it. Think how precious it would be for my little Joanna to play with the same blanket her grandma crocheted as a little girl. Of course it was my first project and the work was elementary. But still she—"

"Annie! Just tell me what you found. We can talk about the afghan later."

"Of course, sorry." Annie set the kettle on Gram's stove and turned on the blue flame beneath. "By the way, I love that jacket. Looks good with your auburn hair. Did Kate Stevens crochet it?" Kate worked at the yarn shop and was an extremely talented designer.

Momentarily diverted, Alice looked down at the burnt-orange jacket trimmed in brown and, maybe realizing she no longer needed the wrap, shrugged it off in the warm kitchen. She hung it across the back of her chair. "You're getting good at spotting the work of the Hook and Needle Club. It is one of Kate's. I saw it on a mannequin at A Stitch in Time and couldn't rest until she agreed to sell it to me. I think it was one of her first. . .hey!" Alice wagged her finger. "You didn't answer me again."

"Would you mind setting up our tea? Then I'll tell you all about my discovery."

"Sure." Alice pulled a favorite tea from the cupboard and pried off the lid. Soon the smell of vanilla almond flooded the room.

"And give Boots some cat food?" Annie asked from the doorway. The cat sat beside her dish, demanding her tea-time treat, too. "I'll go grab my find, and then we can plot our strategy."

"What strategy?" Alice asked.

But Annie didn't seem to hear, disappearing down the

hall.

Alice gave Boots her snack; then she laid out cups and saucers and poured hot water. She pushed the tin of tea bags within reach as Annie returned, carrying the wooden case along with an envelope.

"Aren't these wonderful?"

Alice looked puzzled until Annie explained her discovery, including the theory that Grandpa had carved the patriotic symbols on the case. "Don't you think it's strange? There's already a display case in the living room packed with ribbons and medals. Yet these are kept separate."

"They could belong to someone else," Alice said, dipping a tea bag.

"Otherwise, they'd be displayed with the rest of Grandpa's medals. Wouldn't you think?"

"I would think. It sounds like another attic mystery."

"That's what I thought," Annie said, handing Alice the old photos. "Look at these."

Alice studied them closely. "Who are these people?"

Annie looked doubtful. "I don't know. Don't you?"

"They look like every other old black-and-white I've seen in a picture album. But this one has a certain vintage charm." Alice held out the photo of the couple, hand in hand. "Looks like these two were sweethearts."

Annie sipped her tea thoughtfully, examining the photo again. "She reminds me of Gram as a young woman. But the face is turned and hidden by the hat. Besides, I really don't think this is Grandpa Holden. He was always Gram's one-and-only. So it can't be her."

"Now that's not really the whole story, Annie. Betsy used to say that Charlie Holden may not have been her first love, but he was her true love. Remember?"

Annie sat back. "You're right, Alice. She did say that. In fact, I often thought how lucky I was that Wayne was both my first love *and* my. . .my true love." She swallowed hard.

Alice reached for Annie's arm. "You were very blessed, Annie. You and Wayne both. For many years. Trust me; it doesn't always work out that way."

"I know, Alice. There is so much to be thankful for." Annie hated to say anything that reminded Alice of her divorce. But sometimes. . .well, it hadn't been that long since Wayne's death. Her heart still mourned. Maybe it always would.

"So shall we put our heads together and stitch up a solution for this mystery?" Alice asked, guiding their conversation back to the question of the medals.

Annie took another sip of tea before answering. "I'd love that, Alice. I'm really eager to learn more about the medals. Whether they belong to Grandpa or someone else. Wouldn't it be great to restore them to their rightful owner?"

"No kidding," Alice said. "I'm sure we can figure it out. And there's the Hook and Needle Club, too. They could help."

"They could be a source of information. But I don't want to mention anything about this yet," said Annie.

"Why not? Because they gossip?"

"Well, not really. Although I suppose we need to

consider that." Annie put down the teacup. "I'd like to check around here first. Look through Grandpa's papers and stuff. Find out if there's a reason they wanted them kept a secret. I might be able to find some answers. And there's another reason . . ."

"Oh?" Alice pulled her chair closer to Annie's.

"These things have been hidden away for many years. I'm guessing since the forties. My grandparents kept them a secret for such a long time. They certainly seem to have kept their own family in the dark." Annie put the photographs back in the envelope. "It just makes me wonder why."

"I understand. Caution can't hurt."

"We need to be careful when we share this information."

"Well, sharing information is definitely what we do best in Stony Point," Alice said.

"I have to agree with you there." Annie took hold of Alice's arm, pulling her toward the front door. "And sharing friendship. Come on, we better get going."

*   *   *   *

Entering A Stitch in Time, Annie and Alice found their seats among the other women of the Hook and Needle Club. Annie had already learned that, like in church on Sunday, everyone sat in the same place at the store each Tuesday. She drew her crochet project from her tote bag and started working at once.

"Wow. That's really coming along, Annie. It's going to be gorgeous." Peggy Carson, dressed in a pink waitress uniform, leaned over to take a good look. "Excuse me if I'm jealous, but I don't think I'll ever finish this bed-spread. I tried quilting on my break at the Cup and Saucer but finally figured out the grease stains were changing my color palette."

They laughed, and Annie relaxed into the rhythm of her crochet. She appreciated the new status as an "almost" insider. Maybe someday she would truly be a part of the group.

And of the town.

If she stayed long enough.

"I'd hoped to have it done for the auction, but that doesn't look likely, does it? There's still such a long way to go," replied Annie. "Though I promise I've been working hard."

Annie's afghan consisted of three oversized strips, each with alternating blocks of bulky wool-cotton tweed in four colors: brick red, sunshine gold, purple haze, and chocolate. The pattern called for variegated yarn, but Annie preferred the muted effect of tweed. She feared not having enough brick red. The yarn was hand-dyed and starting a new skein in the middle of a block might not match. If she ran short of yarn, perhaps she could make that block a bit small and the next one more generous.

Stitching again on the last strip, Annie thought of the hours spent last night, attempting to grow the afghan row by row. Instead, her mind had remained occupied with the mystery of the medals rather than completing the crochet project. At least she had the vintage print to donate.

It didn't seem enough. Not for Betsy Holden's granddaughter.

Annie stepped up her stitching speed.

"What's the hurry? It's obvious you won't finish in time. So relax." Mary Beth, owner of A Stitch in Time, pulled up a stool nearby, ready to dash away to help if any customer needed assistance. "Do you have anything else you've made, waiting in the wings, so to speak? Maybe you could donate that instead and save this for another worthy cause."

"What about a baby blanket? Weren't you working on one recently?" Gwendolyn Palmer asked, her knitting needles clicking so fast they almost emitted sparks. "You do beautiful work, Annie. I'm sure your grandmother would approve of such a donation."

Annie looked up, startled. Could she read her mind?

"I did make a couple," she said, "but they're targeted for Texas. For the missionary cupboard at my church. We like to have new things for the missionaries when they come home on furlough." Annie worked three stitches of the red yarn and shifted the strip to start a new row.

Stella Brickson stopped her knitting, "That's very commendable, Annie. It says a great deal about your priorities."

"Maybe it's because my folks were missionaries. I have a little insider knowledge or something." Annie smiled at Stella. "I'd sure feel bad if there were no soft afghans for a young missionary couple home with a new baby. Or maybe to take back into the field."

"But what about the priorities right here in Stony Point?" Peggy said. "We've got plenty of needs. I mean, the church's kitchen needs a new floor at the very least. Have you tried to walk on that thing? It makes me seasick.

And those bathrooms!"

"Let's not go into detail about the bathrooms, Peggy. Not in polite society." Stella barely looked up from her knitting. "Think decorum."

Hearing Stella's remark, Annie hid a grin.

"Wasn't there talk of a new roof?" Mary Beth asked.

"I'm hoping I can get John to get all his banking cronies to take on the roof as a project. After all, the church is used as a community center all week." Gwendolyn warmed to her subject. "Think of how it will benefit all those groups that use the place. The writer's group, the stamp club, the Senior Striders, even that skinny gal who gives those exercise classes, Pilates by Pammy."

"And there's one other group," Alice said, frowning. "I wish I could remember. The name is on the tip of . . ."

"Alcoholics Anonymous?" Peggy asked.

Stella turned her glare toward the waitress, her eyes full of rebuke. Peggy suddenly looked stricken and closed her mouth, forcing her lips into a thin line. She began speed-stitching on her quilt.

The room became quiet. Annie noticed most of the women were covertly looking at Kate, who sat on a stool near the counter. Harry, Kate's ex-husband, was well known for his problems with alcohol.

An uncomfortable silence lingered.

Mary Beth broke it. "Well, anyway, there are sure a lot of diverse groups who count on using the church building, aren't there?"

Eager nods followed. Soon knitting needles began to click again, and they all resumed their chatter.

"Returning to our previous conversation," Gwendolyn said, "Annie, might you consider donating your baby afghans to the auction? Obviously we are a very needy community."

"Let me think about it," Annie said. "Maybe I could send one to Texas and donate one here in Stony Point."

The women murmured their approval, and the room hummed with activity. The store's telephone rang, and Mary Beth jumped up to take it at the counter. But Kate rushed to answer it first, so her boss sat back down. Everyone else carried on.

Gwendolyn spoke over the moving needles. "So. . .any new mysteries up at Grey Gables? Any unidentified pictures? Skeletons in the closet?"

"Not really," Annie said, avoiding eye contact.

The clicking of Gwendolyn's needles stopped. "How exciting! Tell us everything."

"What do you mean tell you everything? I just said no."

Gwendolyn laid her knitting down. "Annie, my dear. You most certainly did not. You said, 'Not really.' "

"Which is pretty much the same as saying, there's more I haven't told you. . .yet," said Peggy, her eyes glittering with interest. "We're ready to help."

"Pardon me?" She glanced over at Alice who sat, staring straight ahead, lost in thought, the cross-stitch in her lap.

"Annie, you've obviously found something and are dangling a mystery in front of us like a carrot, though I can't imagine why," Peggy said, sounding a bit annoyed.

"Oh, do tell us, Annie," Gwendolyn said with a smile.

"Maybe we can help."

"I. . . I. . ." Annie didn't know what to say.

"Wait! I've got it!" Alice said, startling everyone. "The VFW, the Veterans of Foreign Wars." Her attitude seemed triumphant until she saw Annie's alarm. Alice clapped her hand over her mouth.

Annie sat up straight. "Alice!"

"Oh-oh. Alice, you weren't supposed to say that, were you?" Kate had just returned and was watching Annie's reaction to Alice's announcement. "So the VFW has something to do with it. This is getting good."

Alice looked flustered. "No, no! I just meant. . . ah. . .that the Veterans of Foreign Wars also meet at the community center. They really do, every Monday," she said. "Last week, I dropped off a Design Décor calendar kit at the church and set it up for Reverend Wallace. The VFW meeting is listed every Monday for 10:00 A.M."

"Fascinating," Mary Beth said, turning back to Annie. "It's a war mystery then. A foreign war. How intriguing."

"I think you are right, Mary Beth. There's no reason for Annie to be upset unless her secret has just slipped out," Gwendolyn said with a knowing smile.

Annie stared across at Alice. What did she think she was doing?

"That's not what I'm saying. You're jumping to conclusions," Alice protested. She looked at her friend with a helpless expression. "Annie?"

"No comment." Annie sank low in her chair and worked some more stitches. The chatter about the new Grey Gables discovery continued.

What could it be? And which war? Because almost everything in the attic was old, Gwendolyn figured it was a World War II item. Most agreed, except for Peggy, who thought it could be related to Vietnam.

But Annie had to admit they were good. They'd figured out the basis of her secret without much information at all. Maybe she should just tell them. These were persistent women. The mystery might be solved by tomorrow.

Kate was the first to leave, needing to drop off Vanessa at her dad's. Even though the couple had divorced, they tried to be cordial for the sake of their daughter. Annie knew this because, on occasion, Kate couldn't keep her family problems to herself. And Kate's long-suffering relationship with Harry and his alcohol problem was sometimes thrashed about when she wasn't present.

But today there were no post-Kate comments. The ladies were otherwise occupied.

Peggy left moments later, hurrying back to work at the Cup and Saucer.

Annie began to pack up her afghan, which hadn't progressed much because of too many stitches hooked in haste and frustration. She had long been an expert at ripping out rows. Today presented another opportunity to perfect the skill.

Alice, ready to leave, stood by Annie's chair. "Want to have lunch at the Cup and Saucer? I really need to talk to you."

"Fine." Annie narrowed her eyes. "But haven't you talked enough?"

~4~

ustomers crammed the diner as always at this time of day. Alice staked out a messy table and stood guard until Peggy had cleaned it off. They took their seats and waited quietly until Peggy returned with their orders, two heaping plates of three-cheese macaroni, the cook's Tuesday special.

"Just wait until everyone hears what you found in Betsy's attic," Peggy said in a conspiratorial voice, glancing around at the other diners. "A real World War II mystery. Imagine that!"

"Whoa." Annie put up her hand. "Can you rein it in a bit? This is still not public news."

"Oh, now you don't mean that, Annie. You wouldn't deny us a new topic of discussion, would you?" Peggy asked. "It's been pretty dull lately. Back-to-school talk is not all that exciting." She aimed the coffee pot spout toward Alice's mug and poured.

"Please don't talk about this yet, Peggy. Really."

"Why not?" Peggy stopped pouring coffee in midstream.

Annie took a brief look at Alice.

"Trust me," Annie said, turning her attention back to Peggy's question. "I just want a little more time before anyone else learns about it."

Alice had the grace to look embarrassed. "Hate to say so, Annie, but the news is probably all over town by now." She stabbed a mound of cheesy noodles. "This is delicious! Try some before it gets cold."

"I'm afraid Alice is right." Peggy looked concerned. "I expect the details went out over the telephone as soon as you left the yarn shop. Not that anyone is a gossip."

"Good heavens, no." Annie smiled. Actually, everyone in the group was a gossip. But she couldn't hold it against them. They had become quite dear to her in a short time. And she, too, had occasionally been guilty of gossip.

"Tell you what," said Peggy. "I won't say another word about it until you give the green light. Girl Scout's honor," she pledged, giving the three-fingered salute.

"Thanks, Peggy," Annie said. "That's good of you."

"You bet. Anything else I can get you two?" Peggy looked from Annie to Alice and back. "Okay, then. Enjoy your lunch, ladies. Save room for fresh cranberry-apple pie—à la mode."

So that's what smelled so good.

Peggy dashed off to coffee-up more customers. Annie inspected her restaurant plate while trying to decide how best to broach the issue with Alice. Except for the generous portion of mac and cheese, the meal wasn't that interesting. She separated a few cheesy noodles, then took a bite. "Oh. This is delicious!"

"It's great, isn't it? Doesn't even need seasoning." Alice pushed the ceramic cow salt and pepper shakers back behind the napkin holder. Putting her fork down, she leaned forward. "Annie, now that we have some privacy,

I just want to say I'm so sorry about what happened at A Stitch in Time. I never meant to give away your secret."

Alice's earnest apology had an immediate effect on Annie, calming the irritation she had felt. "Oh, I know, Alice. You didn't do it on purpose." Annie sighed. "I just wasn't ready for it to come out yet."

"There had been something in the back of my mind ever since you showed me the medals. Something I should tell you. But I couldn't think what it was," Alice said. "When they started talking about the community groups using the church for a meeting place, I knew that had something to do with it. But I just couldn't quite grasp it."

"And?" Annie helped her along.

"And I then remembered that the VFW meets there every week. They could be players in solving the puzzle. At the very least, maybe they could identify that one medal," Alice said. "But my timing was terrible. I blurted it out right as the women were grilling you. When I realized it. . . well, my panic must have been written all over my face."

"It was, indeed." Annie smiled in sympathy. "In front of anyone else, it wouldn't have been noticed. But not these women. They're like pit bulls with a meaty bone."

Alice laughed. "Pit bulls who make doilies and blankets. Anyway, can you forgive me, Annie?"

"All is forgiven," Annie said, meaning it. "We'll just go forward from here and see what happens. In fact, we ought to stop by that VFW meeting on Monday morning."

"Really?" Alice's expression looked as if someone had

just given her a winning lottery ticket.

"Absolutely. It's a great idea. Who knows what those old heroes can tell us?" Annie grinned and slid aside her plate.

"Now, how about some of that pie à la mode?"

Annie returned to Grey Gables with one keen objective in mind. To search the library for information about Grandpa's military service. On the ride home, curiosity about the medals bubbled in her brain. After Alice dropped her off, she rushed inside, eager to get started.

Boots met her at the front door and leaned hard on Annie's tan twill trousers, a not-so-subtle greeting.

"Did you miss me, Miss Boots?" Annie picked her up for a little cat cuddle, enjoying the purr against her chest. Why hadn't she thought to get a kitty back in Texas? Maybe then she wouldn't have felt quite so alone.

She moved into the living room and arranged an afghan into a little nest, depositing the cat in the center. "How's that? Cozy as can be? Now you take a nice, long cat-nap. I have work to do."

Annie gave Boots one more gentle pat and headed down the hallway toward the library. The sound of paws pouncing on the floor told Annie the short-lived nap had ended. That animal, more like a dog than a cat, always followed her around. Uncanny.

This time, Boots trotted ahead and disappeared into the kitchen. Annie peeked around the corner and saw the cat sitting by her bowl.

"You want food? Again?" Annie pulled the bag of cat food off the shelf and tossed a handful into the empty container. "I don't get how you can eat. I'm stuffed."

The giant slice of cranberry-apple pie had been so sweet, so tart, the crust so flaky, it could have been a contender with Gram's famous peach cobbler. She had eaten every bite. Perhaps she'd better fast through next week.

Annie ambled through the back door and onto the flagstone patio. The soft sea breeze blew a welcome and the azalea bushes swayed like hula dancers. Even the wildflowers, beaten down yesterday by the storm, waved hello in Technicolor pink, purple, and white. Annie's heart swelled. She loved this old place for its peaceful beauty. And because it guarded parts of her past within its winsome walls.

She left the serenity of the lovely landscape behind, went back inside and entered the library. Annie brushed off the back of Gram's favorite chair and sat in her place, remembering. In this room Gram had taught her to crochet while Annie was still a young girl. In this room she often curled up on the window seat and read the classics while Gram created another work of art and Grandpa wrote up James Herriot-type notes from his veterinary practice. Maybe Annie would happen onto them while she was sorting through papers. She smiled. Should be some really good reading. In their family, Grandpa's dog and pony stories were legendary.

The room was lined with rows and rows of shelved books. Along one wall, a handsome oak desk broke the pattern. Annie eyed the desk. On either side were deep file drawers. Maybe that would be a good place to begin her detecting.

Vacating Gram's chair, she crossed to the desk and

opened a deep drawer on the right side. Tabbed files, but not in alphabetical order. No problem. Annie liked a challenge. Hadn't she traveled halfway across the country all by herself? She'd unleashed her inner explorer and she liked it. As she peered into the first file, her pulse raced and a familiar excitement overcame her. A feeling similar to that of walking into a new yarn shop, shelves loaded with undiscovered skeins and never-before-seen patterns. What would she find when she started searching?

Taking a seat in Grandpa's desk chair, Annie had a ridiculous urge to push, toes against floor, and roll across the hardwood until the rug brought her ride to an abrupt halt. Like old times.

What would Gram say?

She would laugh, lift a fist, and exclaim, "Ride 'em, cowgirl!"

Annie pushed off. Gliding over the wood, wheels spinning, she lifted her feet and shouted, "Weeeeeee!" until she came to a sudden stop.

It had seemed a much longer ride when she was ten. But the chair fit her better than before, and she found the brown leather back very comfortable. No wonder Grandpa spent long hours writing at his desk.

Using her feet to walk the chair back, Annie withdrew the first file labeled "bills/statements." She examined the first one, a utility bill. Not too thrilling. Next came telephone, lawn care, life insurance, Malone's Hardware receipts, which reminded Annie that she needed to stop by Malone's and pick out a paint color for the kitchen, plus pay for the charges made by her handyman. She wanted to keep the account current. Gram would expect no less, and for Annie it was a matter of honor.

Beyond the bills were some bank statements dating almost up until Gram's passing. Looking at the official documents, Annie felt a stab to the heart. Like someone stamped "account closed" across her grandmother's life without regard to those who would be left behind.

She sighed. That's the way life is. Even a life lived long seemed too brief.

Putting that file back, Annie chose one labeled "correspondence." Annie knew she should be searching for papers relating to Grandpa Holden's military service, but she wanted to linger in her grandmother's world a bit longer. Opening the file, Annie found dozens of hand-written letters and cards dated over a span of years, each extolling the merit of Betsy Holden's cross-stitch wizardry.

So these were fan letters *to* Gram. Selecting one, Annie read:

> *Dear Mrs. Holden:*
> *I have just finished my third Betsy Original pattern and am so pleased with the outcome! The design is elegant, yet the instructions simple enough that even a beginner . . .*

She smiled as she read to the end and chose another, a more recent thank you card with a personal note inside:

> *Hi Betsy:*
> *Thank you for the cool, cross-stitch class offered through the New England Stitch Club. Though you are a master*

*needle-crafter, you were so helpful and kind. I didn't feel
intimidated at all.*

I'm totally hooked on cross-stitch, thanks to you. . .

The letters were heart warming. So many responses
to Gram's technique and teaching abilities, as well as her
gentle, unassuming nature. Knowing her, every one of
these writers received a response. A Betsy Holden original
letter to file away and keep for always.

Other files held information about investments, car
records, taxes, warranties. Annie opened one marked
"birth certificates." Inside were three certificates:
Gram's, Grandpa's, and one for Judy Elaine Holden,
Annie's mother. Dated 1947 and filled in with her grandparents' names, the baby's place of birth, and other
precious details. Gram often said that having Judy was their
biggest blessing of all.

"She was a blessing to me, too, Gram. And so were
you and Grandpa," Annie said in a prayer-like voice. How
thankful she was to claim such a heritage. Would her
grandchildren feel the same? She put the file back. With
reverence.

Maybe she would find something helpful in the
"mementos" file. Annie opened it, discovering a collection
of clippings from the *Brookfield Star*, her own newspaper
back in Texas. She sorted through them, finding her mom's
and dad's obituaries. Lives ended too soon on the mission
field: her mom's from tuberculosis and her dad's from a
stroke. She had seen the articles many times and put them
back, not wanting to revisit such painful memories.

Surprised, she also found pieces about her own school exploits. Singing in the glee club, tumbling in gymnastic trials, playing flute with the band in the Brookfield Christmas Lights Parade, her senior portrait with her class-mates under the heading "class salutatorian." Graduation from Texas A & M, her engagement photo, marriage announcement, the opening of their dealership and more. Another section filled with keepsakes from LeeAnn's life. Gram had saved them all.

Boots hopped up on Annie's lap, startling her. "You aren't hungry again, are you?" She stroked the cat's velvet coat and checked the desk clock. The files had distracted her for more than an hour. Time to get back to her goal and find some information about Grandpa's military history. She shut the drawer she'd been searching and, leaning over Boots, opened the other side.

There, at the beginning of numerous hanging files, stood a tab marked "Charles Holden—U.S. Navy Records."

— 5 —

Annie carefully removed the narrow folder for further study. She carried Boots and the file into the living room, setting the cat back in the afghan nest. With Annie nearby, Boots closed her eyes and let her head fall against a soft spot. All was well with the feline world.

Annie browsed the file. The papers were crisp and somewhat yellowed, but the typewriter print was clear. The first page looked very official: a Notice of Separation from the U.S. Naval Service: NAVPERS-553. The document provided a concise, official history of Grandpa's military service. Enlistment and discharge dates, schools attended, service vessels and assigned stations, ribbons and medals.

But no Purple Heart.

Annie spotted his discharge pay, a robust $47.78. How had he felt when he mustered out with that paycheck? She shook her head in wonder.

Though not exactly sure what to look for, Annie was quite sure she didn't find it. She would have to examine the document more thoroughly, later.

Or maybe ask someone with sufficient military knowledge to translate the lingo.

Moving on, she found a short dental record, some certificates that indicated Grandpa's specialized training on board ship, and a series of evals: Navy evaluations.

Glancing over them gave her a surge of pride: *unparalleled expertise, excels under pressure*, and *willingly assumes all challenges with enthusiasm and determination*. And her favorite phrase: *already performing at the level of a CPO*. Vintage Charles Holden.

All this, but no mention of a Purple Heart. Or the medal she couldn't identify.

It seemed more and more unlikely that the medals belonged to Grandpa. But why would he take the time and trouble to carve all those intricate designs on the case, if it wasn't his treasured possession?

Annie got up to view Grandpa's medal display, the ones she knew belonged to him. Centered over the shadow box in a triangular case, the American flag folded into the symbolic, tri-cornered shape, featuring only the blue fabric with white stars. Gram had been proud to receive that flag when Grandpa had died, and Annie appreciated its exhibit on his wall of honor.

She remembered Gram giving her a history lesson about the folded flag, explaining its suggestion of a cocked hat. A reminder of the soldiers who once served under General George Washington and of the sailors and marines who served under Captain John Paul Jones. Patriots who paved the way for the U.S. Armed Forces: the men and women who have preserved the freedoms we cherish today.

As Annie focused on the flag, something jogged her memory. Something about the medals she'd found in the attic. One five-pointed star was attached to a blue ribbon. Could there be a connection beyond the obvious

Americana influence? She surveyed the room. Where were those medals, anyway?

Remembering that she had showed them to Alice earlier when they were having tea, Annie strode into the kitchen, deciding she'd take another look at the medals. And maybe she'd better make a cup of tea, as well. A cookie might be nice, but she didn't want to ruin the lingering delight of her Cup and Saucer dessert. Besides, she was still fasting.

For a week.

Or at least until tomorrow.

Annie refreshed the water in the kettle and set it to boiling. She found a sturdy mug and plopped in a tea bag, thinking of all she had learned about her grandparents today. Things she mostly knew, but things worth pondering again. Did her daughter LeeAnn realize her great-gram had kept every newspaper clipping mentioning her name? Every school program? Every card made by childish hands? Annie intended to do the same with her grandchildren.

She sighed and poured hot water into the mug. Taking down a pen and writing tablet, she sat at the kitchen table, pushing the medals away. She could look at them later. Now she wanted to create a new memory. For the twins. And for herself.

Dear John & Joanna. . .

In the late afternoon, Annie sat out on the porch to enjoy the air as she continued her crocheting. Leaning forward she could see the outline of Alice's roof amid the trees nearby. Most likely she wasn't home; she had another home party tonight, this one for Princessa Jewelry. Annie had been invited to come, but she'd replied with an apologetic no. She had all her own jewelry, much of it gifts from her generous husband over the years. And she had inherited all of Gram's jewelry. Annie drew the line at adding any Princessa pretties to her collection.

Gazing at the ocean view, Annie told herself there was nothing like this in Texas. But even as the thought crossed her mind, she felt a kind of disloyalty. She remembered her house in Brookfield, the wildflowers and wide spaces, and her family that waited there. My goodness. She had talked herself into being lonely again. Annie crocheted a few more stitches.

The faraway sounds of gulls soothed her uneasy spirit, calling her to stay in Stony Point for a while longer, anyway. After all, Grey Gables depended on her to restore the beauty it once boasted. That was important. A tribute to her grandmother's memory. Gram had left the house to Annie, and she, in turn, would keep it for those who remained behind.

Besides. . .there were questions to be answered.

No new insights had been gained from inspecting the medals one more time. They were still spectacular. And still mysterious. She didn't think they belonged to Grandpa, not after scanning his file. So who, then? Annie needed help. But not just from anyone, from someone she could trust.

Her crochet hook looped around the bulky brick red

yarn with precision, and the strip grew another half inch. Slow going, but if she stuck with it, the afghan might be finished in time for the auction. She stopped and assessed the rows of even stitches, smiling at the results of her applied skill. What was it about her needlework that filled her with such satisfaction? Annie considered her own question and decided there were too many answers. Perhaps she should return to the real puzzle at hand.

Whom could she call on for help? Alice was already on board. And the Hook and Needle Club was only too eager. But shouldn't Annie find someone with military experience? Mayor Ian Butler might know something about the owner of the medals. He loved Stony Point, making it his business to know the town's history. Even its very recent history. She didn't know if he'd been in the service. That was another question to be answered. But he had become a good friend. Annie trusted him.

Ian could be a great resource.

Annie decided that tomorrow, after paying her charge account at Malone's, she would seek out Ian and enlist his aid.

Right now it was time to put aside her crochet project and go inside.

She had a fast to break.

~ 6 ~

"*L*ook at this Jersey Cream." Annie sorted through scattered paint samples, selecting a multicolored card. "The color's scrumptious!"

Malone's Hardware Store had been the first stop of the day and already much had been accomplished. She had chosen a pattern for the new backsplash though she wasn't sure about the color. Annie liked the antiqued copper look with its depth and earthy tones. But she leaned toward the stainless, as well. The vintage pattern paid tribute to the Victorian style of the house while the silver brought it into the new millennium. She'd have to decide soon.

But she had made a definite decision on appliances. The out-dated machines that now occupied the kitchen would be replaced with shiny new reproductions in the fashion of the late 1800s. The look of the old with the technology of the new. Grandpa and Gram had bought Grey Gables in the late 1940s, choosing it because of the turn-of-the-century architecture. The antique repros complemented the feel of the Victorian style. Annie had chosen the appliances from one of Mike's many catalogs and had only to wait for Wally to take needed measurements to place her order. She would probably get white or black, safe choices that would always be in style. But her inner designer was considering a deep red. What would Gram think of that?

If she went for the red, the stainless backsplash would look amazing. Annie could crochet all new dishcloths to match, some striped, some solid. She might even add crocheted edgings to some store-bought dish towels and give them that vintage feel. Or use some of Gram's cross-stitched towels from the attic.

But the copper was lovely, too.

Oh, what to do. . .what to do.

Annie returned her attention to the Jersey Cream.

"What do you think?" She asked the store owner, holding the paint sample in the light reflected through the store windows.

Mike Malone drummed his fingers against the counter with a let-me-see-now attitude. "You want the truth?"

"Of course." Annie gave him a frank look.

"I don't know what to think," Mike said, suppressing a grin. "Just ask my Fiona. I can be pretty thoughtless sometimes. The important thing is what do *you* think?"

"I think it looks yellow." A voice emanating from the front of Malone's inserted itself into the conversation. Ian Butler, Stony Point mayor, strode a few steps forward and tipped an imaginary hat to Annie who smiled a greeting.

Mike reached out to shake Ian's hand. "Morning, Mayor. How do? You're not here to levy a tax on paint are you? Because, if you are . . ." He gave a good-natured nod toward Annie. "I might have to pass that little hike on to Ms. Dawson here. Not very neighborly of me either."

"What? And bankrupt my constituency?" Ian raised his

eyebrows. "Wouldn't dream of it."

"Well, I'm glad of that!" Annie laughed. "But all teasing aside, gentlemen, I do need to make a decision on this paint. Wally will be ready to paint Gram's kitchen later this week. He started priming the walls before I left the house."

"Then allow me to make a suggestion," the mayor said. "Go with the yellow. You usually aren't sorry if you follow your first inclination." He stopped, as if he'd thought of something significant. "Furthermore, it will accent your sunny disposition."

Annie shook her head. These two were full of it. Whatever *it* was.

"Speaking of accents . . ." Malone pulled more paint samples, shades of white gloss, for Annie's inspection. "One of these for trim?"

"This one," Annie said, pointing to a Winsome White gloss. "And I'll take the Jersey Cream, too. Reminds me of fresh-churned butter."

"Excellent choices, Ms. Dawson. That ought to brighten up your kitchen some. And regarding this paint?" Mike winked and pointed to the can containing the yellow. "Spreads just like butter, too."

Annie rolled her eyes. "I can see I'm not going to one-up either of you. You're too quick for me. We like to take our time back home in Texas."

"You're a good sport, ma'am, and I'll say that for sure." Mike rifled through a drawer until he found an order form. He wrote Annie's selections down, then tossed it back inside. "Tell Wally he can pick up the paint anytime. If he gives me a heads-up, I'll have it mixed and ready to go."

Ian stood by and watched the transaction with apparent interest. Now he made as if to leave, again reaching across to Mike, this time giving him a friendly slap on the shoulder.

"Good to see you, Mike. I have a meeting soon so I need to get back to the office. Give my best to Fiona and the children."

Then, glancing first at his watch, he turned to Annie. "By the way, I wanted to ask you something. Would you mind if we stepped outside for a minute?"

What could the mayor have to ask her? She had a couple things to ask *him*, she knew that much. "Sure," Annie said and walked ahead of him into the sunshine, sandals clacking against the sidewalk. She should have worn more than her sundress and lightweight sweater. The morning was still a bit chilly in spite of the sun.

Ian indicated a wooden bench with wrought iron arms and legs situated a bit south of Malone's. Wine barrels full of vibrant heather decorated either side. The scene was inviting and Annie accepted.

She sat down, turning so she faced the mayor. Annie's impression of Ian was that he seemed to embody the spirit of Stony Point. Rugged, kind, and with a heart for others. The mayor had made her feel welcome when she first arrived, and since then she had always enjoyed his informative talks about the town.

"Please accept my apology, Annie. I've barely time for even a short chat." He checked his watch once more. "It may not surprise you that a rumor about a new discovery at Grey Gables has reached me."

Annie's heart sank. "No, not really," she said. "But it's bizarre, because I already planned to talk to you about it today."

"Great. I'm eager to hear all about it." Ian's eyes sparked excitement. "But that wasn't what I wanted to ask you."

"Oh?"

It was like a mystery leading to the mystery.

"Would you have time to get together later this afternoon?" Ian started to rise. His mayoral duties called. "How about we meet in the town square?"

Annie thought about the day ahead. She might need to stop by A Stitch in Time and check out their cotton yarn, just in case she decided to make those red dish cloths. Or another color, if she chose the copper backsplash. Any visit to her very favorite shop could take hours, depending on who was present. Topping her list was a visit to the Stony Point Library to try and get information about Grandpa.

If she did discover new information, she would have it in hand to discuss with the mayor. He might be able to offer advice.

"How about three o'clock?" Annie asked, standing.

"Let's synchronize our watches," Ian said, checking his again. He laughed at his little joke. "All right, then. I'll meet you at three over by Old Glory. I'll bring coffee."

They said their good-byes, and Ian turned and walked rapidly toward the town hall. He took the time to wave or exchange a word with several Stony Point citizens, until he cut across the square's lush lawns and disappeared.

Musing, Annie crossed Main Street and sauntered toward the yarn shop, enjoying the leisurely pace, returning the smiles of those she met along the way. She knew many of these folks now. And most of them knew her. Or of her. Gram had been integral to this community, and Annie loved claiming the heritage. An unexpected gift.

In front of A Stitch in Time, she paused, taking in the picture-postcard feel of the village that was Stony Point. She touched the cool metal lamppost situated outside the shop and remembered swinging around and around one like it during her childhood. Probably every child in town had done the same. And she loved to see those lamp lights lit, lending enchantment to the night, beaming in rows, and marking a path through town. Like tiny replicas of Butler's Lighthouse, showing strangers the way.

Only I am a stranger no more.

Annie hugged herself, just for a moment. Then, heart smiling with contentment, she stepped into the shop.

~ 7 ~

When Annie exited more than an hour later, she carted two bulky bags along with her purse. It was a blessing she didn't have a charge account at A Stitch in Time, or she might have needed help to carry her riches to the car. She had bought plenty of red cotton yarn, and also white, so she could have more options.

But that didn't mean she'd decided for sure on the red appliances. Annie also purchased some soft skeins of butter-yellow. In case of copper. The white would work with either scenario.

Heading around the corner toward her trusty old Malibu—a gift from Wayne she still couldn't bear to sell—Annie realized she was building another stash right here in Stony Point. Back in Brookfield, an entire bedroom was set aside and dedicated to conserving her collection of crochet yarn. And hooks. And patterns. And unfinished projects. Somehow the stash had grown beyond the bedroom, multiplying like rabbits on the Texas plain.

Maybe she'd just have two stashes. A Texas stash and then. . .her *Maine* stash.

Annie loaded her bags into the trunk then opened the passenger door to retrieve Grandpa's military file tossed on the seat before she left Grey Gables that morning. It had taken more than a few weeks to relax and learn to leave car doors unlocked like the rest of Stony Point. Now she reveled in trusting her neighbors and friends with her property.

A gentle breeze blew the scent of brine into the center of town, and Annie breathed deep, reminded of the town's rich history. She pulled her sweater close and wandered past the shops, trying to visualize the first trading post back in 1665. Could those early settlers have known they were building a community that would still thrive more than three hundred years later?

As she rounded the corner onto Main Street, Annie peeked through the windows of Dress to Impress, the women's clothing store. She could have used a few of those stunning outfits when she worked with Wayne at the dealership. What did she have to dress up for now?

As she passed near the Cup and Saucer, the aroma of culinary delights wafted her way, reminding her she had skipped lunch. A glance at her watch showed she had less time to research Grandpa's file than planned.

She wouldn't stop to eat. Instead, she picked up her pace and hiked over to the Stony Point Library. Stopping on the sidewalk allowed her to appreciate the Greek-revival-temple-style structure built in the 1840s, originally a private home. The library, with its stark white paint, stately columns, and black shutters, held its own among other prominent buildings on Main Street. A mix of dignified nobility and colonial charm. Very New England.

She climbed the steps to the pillared porch, hesitating in front of a multipaned glass door. What would she find out about Grandpa? About the medals? Did she really want to know?

Grasping the handle, she pulled the door open. As she stepped inside, the familiarity of the foyer flooded over her. How many times had she come here with Gram to check out a Nancy Drew mystery or Black Stallion book?

On the wall to the right hung a framed photograph of an older woman, smiling, against a backdrop of shelved books. Below her picture an engraved brass plate read: Josephine Booth, Library Volunteer of the Year. One might have expected to see the head librarian or some staff photos, but in Stony Point, it didn't surprise her to see volunteers celebrated first.

Annie inhaled the smell of polished wood and old books while creeping into the Great Room. Two teen-aged girls, seated in oak Windsor chairs surrounding an oval table, typed away on laptops. Then one stopped and showed something on her screen to the other, who giggled. An older man wearing a plaid shirt and suspendered jeans sat nearby, flipping through a magazine with a blue plastic cover. It all looked much the same as Annie remembered from her childhood visits. The sun streaming through tall windows, white shelving all around, and Currier & Ives prints of ancient sailing vessels grouped above the fireplace mantel.

But to Annie, everything appeared small scale. The Great Room seemed like a cathedral when she was a girl. Now it was simply a large, lovely room. Like a two-page spread out of an old *Architectural Digest*. Though, to her way of thinking, the picture wouldn't include the constant tapping on keyboards. Or the steady snores from a young man asleep in a comfy chair across the room, his leg draped over its arm.

As Annie approached the Circulation Desk, someone pushed a book truck down an aisle and disappeared into the stacks with the load. Could that have been Josephine? Maybe. Hard to tell from the back view.

Annie noticed several informational signs posted around the area: "We have wireless!" "Don't forget story time every Friday from 10 to 11 A.M." and, "It's not too late to take a vacation with us. A new Armchair Traveler Tour begins next week." She remembered how Gram always used to call her library card a "Passport to Adventure."

Behind the desk, a petite woman with a boyish figure set aside a bunch of books to check in. She seemed young, her brown hair streaked with blond highlights and cut in a short style. But as Annie drew nearer, she could see the woman's lined face and quick hint of a smile that, while friendly, didn't quite light up the wide, blue eyes. The only sparkle in her expression came from her diamond earring studs.

"How may I help?" She widened her smile and gave Annie her attention. A name badge identified the woman as Grace Emory, Reference Librarian.

"I actually do need some help, Miss. . .ah. . ." Annie eyed the wedding band on the librarian's left hand. "I mean, Mrs. Emory."

"Call me Grace," she said, speaking in a brisk, no-nonsense tone. As if either very anxious to help Annie, or equally eager to help her right out of the building.

Annie decided to go with the first option.

But maybe she needed to try an ice-breaker question.

"Grace," Annie started, "was that Josephine I saw

pushing a cart full of books up and down the rows?"

A pleased look flashed across Grace's face, almost extending to her eyes. "You know Josephine?"

"Well, I don't really know her, except from the picture in the foyer. But I thought it sweet that you honored her with that spot out there, where everybody can see. She must feel appreciated."

"She *is* appreciated. One-hundred-percent and then some." Grace gave a quick nod. "So what are you looking for?"

To Annie, the woman still seemed stiff. Inhibited.

Time for icebreaker number two.

"My goodness. I can't help but notice those beautiful diamond earrings. They are just exquisite," Annie said.

Grace's eyes misted. "Thanks. A gift from my husband for our thirty-fifth." She touched the earrings, as if to check and be sure they were still in place.

"He sounds like a keeper to me," Annie said, grinning. "Just imagine what he'll get you for your fortieth!"

"I do imagine it. All the time." Grace blinked away mounting tears. "Won't happen though. Don passed away. Cancer."

Annie caught her breath. "I'm so sorry! Please forgive me. I had no idea. . ."

"Of course not." Grace returned to her professional brisk self. "It hasn't been very long."

"No wonder you are so sensitive. I do understand. How long has it been?"

"Five years."

Five years? And Grace still so overcome with grief?

It had been a year since Wayne passed. The hardest year of Annie's life. But she clung to the hope that the black cloud of sorrow would continue to fade day by day—like a fog turning into mist, then vanishing into a memory. Was she fooling herself?

The conversation Annie initiated almost made her forget why she'd come. But the file served to bring her back on course. To find any written record of Grandpa's military service beyond the forms she had discovered in his desk.

She showed Grace the file, pointing to the separation paper in particular and explained finding some medals in her grandmother's attic and wondering if they belonged to her grandfather. It occurred to Annie then, she had spilled more of the mystery in the attic than had Alice. Would that make a problem with the Hook and Needle Club? What if one of them found out she had given Grace the information Annie had not trusted them with? Her friends who so wanted to know the details? Not that she was worried about Grace. She was a professional.

But still. . .

This may have been a big mistake.

Hindsight. And that twenty-twenty vision thing.

"So you must be Betsy's granddaughter! I have something to show you later," Grace said. "But about your grandfather. We have wonderful archives of *The Point*, our local newspaper, going back to the first issue. All on microfiche. I think that's where we should start."

Since Grace and Josephine were covering all the public desks while the other two employees were at lunch, the librarian put out a sign alerting patrons to push a red button for service. Then Grace grabbed the beeper and led Annie through an archway and into the Reference Room.

The area was the opposite of the gracious Great Room. On one side stood the reference collection in printed format. Books. On the other, computer stations backed one another in two rows of ten each. Most were filled with youngsters, engaged in their e-mails or games and focusing hard on their monitors. A few other patrons seemed to be doing serious research.

Annie thought any activity attempted must have a better outcome here with help from this knowledgeable staff. Excited that the mystery had brought her here today, she wondered what stories and facts waited to be discovered. Maybe about her own family. She couldn't wait to get started.

"We have access to millions of magazine and newspaper articles through our library databases. Great resources," Grace said. She seemed to have warmed to the subject of her beloved library. "Unfortunately, what you're seeking isn't online. Or indexed."

"Oh-oh. That sounds like more work for me," Annie said, sitting down in front of a large microfiche/microfilm reader-printer. She remembered using one of these in college, but goodness, that had been a long time ago.

"Sorry. One day, we hope to have all these materials indexed. The Historical Society's been considering the project. That won't help you now." Grace had grown animated, talkative. "Sometimes, you just have to start at the beginning."

She flipped the "on" switch, and the machine's inner

workings fired up with a thunk, sounding like a faulty automatic transmission slipping into gear. But in spite of the noise, the unit didn't move or shudder and didn't resist when Grace threaded the fiche through the mechanisms, giving Annie a quick demo. Soon, a special edition of *The Point* from August 14, 1945, appeared on the screen. "War Over! Victory Declared!" accompanied by a picture of President Harry Truman making the official announcement to a large gathering of reporters in the White House.

"We have an original copy of this issue in the Stony Point Museum. Under glass."

"Wow. I'd like to see it sometime," Annie said, looking up at Grace. "But this is almost as good." Turning back to the page display, she saw several front-page stories about the end of the war. Annie worked the knobs, manipulating the image on the screen and going on to the next.

"Work backward. See if there's any mention of your grandfather. I did notice he's originally from. . .where?" Grace referred to the separation paper. "Right, High Falls, Connecticut. Shall I initiate an interlibrary loan for you? It's more likely that his hometown paper would have the information you want."

Annie was pretty sure that Grace's eyes twinkled a bit from interest in the subject and not just a reflection of those diamond earrings.

"Thanks so much." She watched Grace move off to the reference desk and work on the staff computer, busying herself with the request.

After examining a roll of fiche, Annie realized this

would be a long process. There were years of newspapers to peruse, an impossible task to rush. It was simply too interesting. All the stories, the history of the town, the names she recognized.

And the ads. She especially enjoyed all the sales advertised for Bascom's Department Store. Annie had often visited Bascom's with Gram during her summer visits. Those were cherished times, especially since the store had gone out of business years ago.

She would need a lot more time than a couple hours one afternoon at the Stony Point Library. The wall clock said it was getting close to 3:00 P.M. Annie reversed the fiche and, when it stopped spinning, placed the roll into its proper box. Not sure what to do with all the boxed rolls still unsearched, she piled them together by date and left them on top of the machine.

Josephine would have to clean up the mess, poor thing.

Annie decided to explore more of the library on her way out, so she wandered through the reference stacks, looking at the titles of various encyclopedias, directories, and analogs. A person could really lose herself in all this information. She rounded one of the rows and came face-to-face with a familiar, yet shocking sight.

One of Gram's lovely cross-stitches.

Framed in dark cherry wood with a navy-colored mat, the seascape pictured Butler's Lighthouse soaring above the horizon at the end of the point, ready to guide weary sailors into safe harbor. Annie had watched Gram stitch this piece one summer after an incident involving a local fishing boat during a storm. One soul was lost that day, but many men were saved by the light from Stony Point's only Lighthouse. Gram stitched her sadness and her gratitude right into the fabric. And created a masterpiece.

"I see you found it yourself." Grace had come up behind Annie, startling her. "Superb, isn't it?"

"I was visiting the summer she made it. I remember how moved she was by the tragedy, though it could have been much worse. See? In the corner? She stitched the name of the man lost at sea."

Grace nodded. "We're proud to have it in our art collection. It's kept in the rare book case to protect it, to keep it from fading. And also, it just happens to be displayed right by the needlecraft section."

"The perfect place for a Betsy Original."

"Exactly." Grace returned the file used to send Annie's interlibrary loan request. "I've already turned over your ILL to Valerie Duffy, our circulation and interlibrary loan librarian. She'll see it through. Though it might take a couple weeks to get an answer from Connecticut. Hope there's no rush."

"No. No rush." Annie glimpsed the wall clock.

Except right now.

She waved her thanks to Grace. And with file in hand, Annie rushed toward the town square.

~ 8 ~

*B*reathless, Annie arrived at the town square with six minutes to spare. The wind had picked up a little, causing her to pull her sweater tighter as she hurried across Main Street. Not so easy when she was also speeding in sandals and trying to be sure Grandpa's papers didn't fly out to sea. Her tousled locks whipped around her face. Feeling a little light headed, as if someone had emptied all her energy into the morning and left none for the afternoon, she dropped down onto a bench.

The sound of Old Glory snapping in the wind gave her a patriotic jolt as she waited for Ian. Annie's thoughts turned to how he had shepherded her through the Fourth of July fireworks after Alice had slipped away to find a friend. Ian made a clumsy situation seem quite natural with his offer of lawn chairs under the stars. Annie had been grateful to sit and watch the stunning display of lights exploding against the night sky.

Stony Point seemed to awaken her sleeping patriot within. All the historical points of interest and artifacts—and even watching the fishermen cast out to sea each day—made Annie feel connected to her nation's roots. Maybe she'd crochet an Americana something—or develop a simple project for Mary Beth's children's table at next year's Fourth festivities.

Next year? The thought gave her pause. One thing for sure, she'd better stay out of Gram's attic or she would never get back to Texas.

"I brought sustenance," Ian said, appearing suddenly and interrupting Annie's thoughts. He handed her a tall paper cup with a lid. "Coffee, to start."

"Mighty Mayor has come to save the day. Thank goodness!" Annie said, smiling. The hunger she had denied earlier returned at the first fragrance of coffee and. . . what else?

"Hope you don't mind leftovers," he held the bag in front of her. "Thought you might need a pick-me-up about now."

"You must be a mind reader." She peered into the bag. "Where did these come from?"

"A lunch meeting. My secretary ordered them from the Cup and Saucer." The mayor sat beside Annie. "She knows how to pamper us. Apricot-pecan scones. Try one."

Annie took a bite and chewed. "Mmm. Heaven!" She sipped her coffee, savoring the rich flavor. "Thanks."

Between swigs of coffee, Ian made a few comments about the weather and tossed out pleasantries, giving Annie a chance to finish her scone. When she refused another, he folded the sack of scones and said, "So, tell me about the mystery in the attic."

Energized by her mini-lunch, which did, after all, contain fruit and nuts, Annie explained about finding the medals. Drawing air pictures, she described each one and the patriotic carving on the case, as well.

"I'm pretty sure it's Grandpa Holden's handiwork.

But what I can't figure out is why he spent hours whittling the wooden case unless the medals were his. I mean, that doesn't make sense, does it?"

"No, not at this point," Ian agreed. "Let me see if I have the facts straight. You found two medals. One is a Purple Heart, right?"

Annie nodded. "I don't know what else it could be."

"And the other is gold and looks like a sheriff's badge?"

"Sounds silly, doesn't it? But that's what I thought when I first saw it." She shrugged. "Or like the toy badge kids wear when they play cowboys."

Downing more coffee, the mayor looked off into the distance, as if he was searching through a mental database. "Do you remember seeing any printing on the medal? Like maybe the word "valor"?

"Not that I remember. It's a five-pointed star hanging on a blue ribbon. The clasp part is decorated with white stars."

"Were the stars lined up in a chevron pattern?"

Annie gave him an exasperated look. "I don't know. . . maybe." She sipped her coffee and eyed the folded sack, thinking about the other scone inside.

"Are you warm enough? Want my jacket?" Ian indicated his lightweight navy blazer, apparently ready to pull it off if Annie was chilled.

She smiled. "I'm fine, thanks, Mayor. The coffee warmed me right up."

"Good." He sat back on the bench. "Okay, we have one identified medal and one mystery medal. Anything else?"

"This." Annie opened her grandfather's file, taking out the Notice of Separation from the U.S. Naval Service. "This form shows some of the medals he received, and a Purple Heart wasn't among them."

"You're right." Ian scanned the paper. "Interesting. I haven't seen one of these before."

"Really?" Annie leaned over to look again. "I would think every serviceman would be given one when he—or she—gets out of the military."

"Right again. But this particular form wasn't used when I was discharged. We used a DD 214. This is a NAVPERS-553. But it's similar."

"Do you think that has some significance?" Annie asked.

"Probably not. Just proves it's old." Ian said, a grin lighting up his blue eyes. "But we knew that already, right? It's your grandpa's."

Annie showed him the rest of the file containing the evaluations, dental records, and certificates. Ian didn't look all that impressed.

"It looks like he was a hospital apprentice and then later a pharmacist's mate. Though," his bland expression turned to one of interest, "that second rating would put him aboard a ship." He scanned the page. "Yep. Right here. Your grandpa served aboard a hospital ship, the USS *Beneficent*. Right near the action, too."

"Grandpa had already taken some college science classes when he enlisted. He was preparing to become a veterinarian. I like the idea he was taking care of other soldiers and sailors on the ship. It sounds just like him."

Ian nodded. "He was a great vet. Saved our old spaniel once. We almost lost him, but thanks to Dr. Holden, Brutus was with us several more years. Your grandpa was a hero in our family."

"Thanks for telling me that." Annie's eyes misted. "He was a great man. Sure wish I'd paid more attention when he talked about his military service." She sighed. "Of course, he didn't talk about it much. Maybe it was a guy thing."

The mayor glanced at her. "Possibly. Or he figured it wasn't a kid thing."

The explanation made sense to Annie. Grandpa Holden had always been more compelled to converse about her cares than dwell on his own.

"Sorry, but the rest of this information, while memorable, doesn't seem to hold any clues to your mystery. Except to affirm the medals you found are not your grandfather's."

"That's what I thought, too." Annie's face fell for a moment. Then she remembered her library visit. "I just talked to Grace Emory, and she got me started searching *The Point* on microfiche from the day World War II ended and going backward."

"That sounds positive. Grace knows her stuff. What did you find?"

"Well. . .nothing that would help the hunt. So far, anyway. I got lost in the personal stories. And in the ads!" Her face brightened. "I could scroll through those for hours."

"What did you find?"

"There was one about making sure your stocking

seams are straight to keep your husband happy. And it was an ad for Lux detergent!" Annie laughed. "Oh, and Reese's peanut butter cups: a pack of twenty-four for five cents."

Ian shook his head. "It's a new day. No doubt about it." He handed the file back to Annie. "Do you have anything else relating to the medals? Letters? Pictures?"

Annie clasped her hand over her mouth and then removed it, saying, "Oh, that's right!"

"What is it?"

"I can't believe I forgot," she said. "I have pictures, too."

"Tell me," Ian said.

She told him about the black-and-white photos at the bottom of the box that housed the medals. "The young woman reminds me of Gram when she was very young. Just a little. But I can't tell for sure, because she's not facing the camera. And she's wearing a hat, too."

"Could it be your grandparents?"

"I'm pretty sure the man isn't my grandfather. So it's probably not them." Annie looked thoughtful as she finished off her coffee. "Though Gram had a sweetheart before she met Grandpa. So. . .?"

"This could be him?" Ian asked.

"It's possible, I guess. But who is he? How will I find out? There are no names on the back."

The mayor had a ready answer. "Stella Brickson. They were friends when Stella was a young girl, right?"

"Of course! Now I'm excited!"

"Glad to help. I might be of more assistance if I could actually see the medals. Do you think you could drop them by the office one of these days?"

"Yes." She thought a moment. "Maybe I should try and speak to Stella first. She might have information that would fill in some blanks."

"Good idea." Ian stood. "Feel free to call or drop by my office any time that's good for you. If I'm not there, just leave a message with Mrs. Nash. I'll be in touch."

"I can do that." Annie started to rise also. "By the way, at Malone's you said there was something you wanted to ask me. What is it?"

"I'm afraid you'll think it odd," he said, hesitating, "but I wanted to ask if I could borrow Wally to paint my kitchen sometime in the next year or so. I know you've got him tied up pretty well out at Grey Gables. But there are other people interested in hiring him. People in local government, even."

"Mr. Mayor!" Annie acted indignant, but inwardly she chuckled. "Are you using your official title to make me give up my handyman?"

"Would it help?"

"No. But I'll lend him to you, anyway, right after my kitchen is done. How's that?"

"It's a bargain. Now I need a little advice on a paint color . . ."

— 9 —

*I*an escorted Annie back to her car before returning to his office. She was eager to quiz Stella. This morning she had been knitting in her favorite chair at A Stitch in Time. Might she still be there?

Annie opened the car door and dropped the file on the back seat. Then she dashed around the corner, hoping to see Stella inside.

Peering past the stenciled store name on the front window, she saw Alice instead, standing at the counter. She seemed to be sorting through a big basket of patterns. Annie entered and walked up to her friend. "Are you spending more of your hard-earned money in here?"

"She's got to spend it somewhere," Mary Beth said. "Might as well be here. And here and here and here." She tapped several patterns that Alice had chosen from a basket labeled "Sale—20% Off."

"Just doing my part to keep the economy going," Alice said. "Look, Annie. I actually found a Betsy on sale! I can't pass it up." She pushed one of the patterns toward her friend.

"I'm telling you, Alice, that's a mistake," Mary Beth said. "I never mark down Betsy's cross-stitch patterns. Don't have to. They sell themselves." She gave Alice an accusatory glare. "Are you sure you didn't put that pattern in the sale basket yourself?"

"I won't dignify that question with any other answer than this: You watched me sort through these patterns, Mary Beth. One by one. Why, Betsy herself used to say 'Patience is a virtue.' " And I *was* patient, searching for the perfect pattern. You know the Betsy Original was in this bunch." Alice continued flipping through the patterns. "Don't blame me for your mistake."

"Alice has a point," Annie smiled. "Besides, isn't the customer always right?"

Mary Beth released a big sigh. "Fine! But I'm watching you." She pointed to Alice. "Twenty percent off and not a penny more."

"What about my discount for bringing you a hamburger last week?"

"Don't push it." Mary Beth walked over to a wall displaying all manner of patterns and how-to books for knitting, crocheting, quiltmaking, scrapbooking, and of course cross-stitching. "I'll be over here guarding my stock if you need me."

Annie picked up the Betsy Original pattern that Alice slid across the counter. Titled "The Sanctuary." Not Gram's typical design. It showed a country church with spire stitched against a plain background, no clouds or horizon. The pristine white of the building, bordered by lacy trees, gave the impression of a free-floating, shaded structure embossed on the blue aida cloth.

The little church could be floating on a blue-gray sea as the fog rolled in, like a sanctuary spot in the storms of life. Or perhaps it wasn't grounded on earth at all but set in the sky and lifted far above the fray, ever higher toward heaven.

Gram had created an elegant design meant to inspire the viewer. And she succeeded. Alice soon selected the sale items she wanted, paid Mary Beth, and the two friends headed outside. Alice hugged the package. "I can't believe my luck! A Betsy Original. And such an unusual one, too. Have you seen this one before?"

Annie admitted she couldn't recall that particular pattern. But there were so many.

As the two strolled across Main Street and onto Oak Lane, Alice asked, "Where have you been all day? I think I filled up your message machine, trying to get hold of you."

"Oh, here and there." Annie explained her whereabouts, adding details about her trip to the Stony Point Library and her chat with Ian. "He had a great suggestion about the mystery, too. Don't you think it's helpful to discuss things with Mayor Butler? He's able to pull all the facts together and give a clearer picture. Cut through the baloney, so to speak."

"A good trait in a mayor. What did he say?" Alice asked.

"One thing in particular, about those photos. He said I should talk to Stella. Maybe she could give me some answers."

"He's right. We know she was devoted to Betsy when they were young." Alice stopped. "Hey. Didn't I say the same thing to you?"

"Did you?" Annie asked as they approached her car. "When?"

Alice gave an impatient sigh. "Yesterday morning. Remember? I told you we should get the Hook and Needle Club involved."

Annie looked baffled for a moment; then her face cleared. "Well, of course you did."

"Thanks. Just trying to get some credit here," Alice said.

Annie tossed her arm around Alice's shoulder and gave her an impromptu hug. "No worries. Your credit is always good with me."

Then she dug in her purse for her car keys. "I better get home. Wally's been working in the kitchen, and I'm dying to see what he's done. Plus, I have all those messages to listen to on my answering machine. Why were you calling me, by the way?" Annie asked.

A shadow passed over Alice's face. "Well, I still feel bad about giving out too much information about the medals. I'd like to make it up to you. How about I take you out to dinner at the Fish House?"

"The Grand Avenue Fish House? I've never been."

"One and the same. We can have a ladies' night. Dress up and enjoy ourselves. Swap stories about Stony Point. It will be fun. Let's do it."

"Tonight?"

"Why not? We both have to eat. And there's plenty of time. Say yes."

All of a sudden, Annie couldn't think of anything she wanted to do more. "Yes!"

*   *   *   *

Later that evening, Annie shut the driver's side door and moved away from the Malibu, brushing any imaginary dust from her favorite floral-print dress. She'd added a black velveteen jacket for warmth and punctuated her look with jet earrings, a birthday present from the twins last Christmas. She felt full of anticipation. How sweet Alice had been to think of this evening out.

Annie gazed at her friend, admiring how good she looked in her deep brown retro dress. Alice looped elbows with Annie. "Let's go have a nice dinner and enjoy our evening. We deserve it."

They walked into the Grand Avenue Fish House and were seated right away, thanks to Alice's foresight to make a reservation. The view from their table was magnificent as the last of the twilight sky vanished with the sun. The stars glittered and the sea shimmered, quiet and peaceful this night. They could even see Butler's Lighthouse in the distance, which gave Annie a feeling of security. And a pinch of nostalgia, too, since viewing Gram's cross-stitch earlier today.

A young man with slicked-back hair brought them stemmed goblets of ice water and handed each a leather-covered menu. "Good evening, ladies. My name is Derek, and I'll be your waiter. May I recommend the house special?"

"You may," Alice said. "Pray, enlighten us."

Annie opened and studied the menu. In her opinion, Alice was acting like the lady-of-the-manor. Best to avoid eye contact.

"Certainly. Tonight we have a Mediterranean seafood stew with Maine lobster, shrimp, sea scallops, blue mussels, littleneck clams, and a smokehouse almond-basil pesto." Derek had every line memorized. "May I start you off with something from the bar?"

Annie and Alice declined Derek's offer, opting instead for the water.

"Are either of you interested in the special?"

"Sounds delightful. But I'd like to look at your other selections before I decide," Alice said, opening her menu.

"Me, too." Annie appreciated the amazing fresh seafood available here on the coast of Maine, but the special featured a lot of fishy flavors in one dish. Especially for a Texas-barbeque-kind-of-gal. "Thanks."

"Isn't this fun?" Alice leaned forward. "I can't imagine why we don't do this once a week. I feel so. . .so. . .fancy!" Her blue eyes flashed with apparent pleasure.

Annie smiled her agreement. She surveyed the room, taking in the gleaming wood floors, the soft overhead lighting, and round tables—most situated in front of the wall of windows facing the harbor where spectacular scenery dominated the décor. Its only adornment, a gold-rimmed hurricane lamp at the center of each table—candlelight flickering inside the glass. The effect reminded Annie of a plain black dress worn with a diamond pendant. The perfect accessory.

Alice gave an understated wave. "Look who's here!"

"Who?" Annie searched the diners until she saw one waving back. "Why it's Kate and Vanessa. And who is that with them?"

"Kate's former husband, Harry Stephens." Alice lowered her voice as if their conversation might be heard several tables away. "He's a handsome man. No wonder Vanessa is such a beautiful girl. Kate looks lovely, doesn't she?"

Annie nodded. "Yes. I can't imagine why Harry would

let her get away."

"I really don't know him at all, but everybody knows about his problem. I hear he's really sweet except when he's drinking. And he often is."

"I've heard some snippets at the Hook and Needle Club. Not a lot, just that he drinks too much and goes kinda crazy," Annie said, regret in her voice. "It must be hard for Kate. And for Vanessa. I can't imagine raising LeeAnn without Wayne there to parent with me."

"Lots of women do it," Alice said. "Look. Here comes Vanessa. Doesn't she look grown up tonight?"

As Vanessa approached, Alice's expression took on a look of longing.

Was this a hidden heartbreak? That Alice had no child of her own?

"Vanessa, you look so pretty tonight. What a beautiful shawl. Another of your mom's originals?" Alice asked.

"It's cool, isn't it?" Vanessa said, shy pride in her voice.

"She made mine, too." Alice pulled her cream-colored wrap off the back of her chair. "I love it."

"Sweet." The teen twirled around for them and the long fringe flew out, hitting the back of Annie's chair. "Oops. Sorry."

Annie waved away the apology. "Come closer and let me look at that piece of art you are wearing. Your mom is a genius." The black lacy pattern embellished with hot pink crocheted rosettes complemented Vanessa's pink party dress. And in the usual Kate Stevens style, the work was exquisite.

"I know. She makes me lots of things. All the girls at school want to be me." Vanessa preened a little, turning from side to side, allowing the fringe to float. "This one is a present. Today's my birthday." She flushed and broke into an infectious grin.

"Happy birthday!" Annie and Alice both burst out their salutations in unison. "So this is your birthday dinner with your folks?" Annie asked.

"Yeah." Vanessa looked back at her family's table and waved. "My mom was just telling my dad how you've become a member of the Hook and Needle Club, Mrs. Dawson. And," the teen paused, as if for effect, "I told him you solved mysteries, too."

Annie laughed. "That's a generous statement, Vanessa. You make me sound like a TV heroine."

"I bet you could be one—if you had a TV show," Vanessa said. "Mom told us that you found a World War II secret in your grandmother's attic. Is that true?"

Inwardly, Annie groaned. But before she could answer that unwelcome question, the waiter appeared at the table to take their orders. Vanessa made her excuses, saying she'd better get back to her parents. First she leaned over and whispered to Annie, "You should try the garlic shrimp. It rocks."

Derek turned to Annie, poised to record her wishes to memory. Because she'd had no time to look at her menu, she said, "I'll have the garlic shrimp, please." If a fifteen-year-old girl said it rocked, it must be fabulous.

"The grilled rainbow trout," Alice announced, closing her menu with a snap and handing it back to Derek. "My favorite."

The friends sat back in upholstered chairs and peered out into the night. This had been a good idea.

"You know, Alice, there's only one thing that could make this evening even better," Annie said with a little smile.

"What would that be?"

"If we could work on our needlework projects while we wait."

Alice raised her eyebrows. "You know what that means, don't you, Annie?"

"No, what?"

Alice sighed wistfully. "That we're getting old."

"Almost," Annie said. "We won't be truly old until we want our slippers, too."

They laughed and continued in easy conversation until a noise from across the room caused them to stop. Raised voices came from the Stevens' table. Couldn't they get through the evening without an argument? And on their daughter's birthday, too? Vanessa sat looking down at her plate, all her joyful expression gone. Annie tried to concentrate on the seaside view, but the voices grew louder and louder. With a screech, Harry pushed his chair backward and stood. He tossed some bills on the table, leaned over, and gave his daughter a brief kiss on the forehead. Then rushing past the table where Annie and Alice sat, threw a withering glance their way and ran from the restaurant.

Within minutes, Kate had called for the check, placed the bills inside the payment folder, and ushered Vanessa toward the exit. As they walked past Annie's table, Kate gave Annie a chilly glare.

Annie caught her breath. What had she done?

— 10 —

"Excuse me, but what was that all about?" Alice asked incredulously as Derek placed their salads on the table.

"I have absolutely no idea." Annie was as mystified as her friend. "Could I have hurt Vanessa's feelings somehow? I sure didn't mean to." She picked up her salad fork and, shaking her head, speared a lettuce leaf.

"I don't see how. It must have been a look left over from Kate's encounter with Harry."

"Didn't you say he was sweet? Except when he was drinking?" Annie asked. "He didn't look drunk to me."

"You probably couldn't tell if he was," Alice responded. "But he is nuts about Vanessa."

"Then why fight on her birthday?"

"Sometimes it seems . . ." Alice's words drifted off as she became lost in her reflections.

"What?" Annie asked. "Seems like what?"

Alice appeared to choose her words with care. "Well, I've lived here a long while and heard quite a bit of the Stevens' history. And I hate to say it, but it's almost as if there's a black cloud over that family."

"I don't understand," Annie said.

"I think it's a generational thing. From father to son to

grandson. Harry's the third in line to inherit the alcoholic habit."

Annie swallowed a mouthful of crisp greens before speaking. "So they all had a drinking problem? Poor Vanessa."

"Well, that might be overstating it a bit. As I understand it, the grandfather had a terrible problem when he was a young man, but he quit. His son Robert stays sober through a twelve-step program and has worked the family fishing business ever since."

"And this is the heritage Kate married into? Didn't she think about that?"

"You know how love is," Alice said. "Visually impaired and all. Been there myself." She stabbed a cherry tomato with gusto.

Or maybe anger. Annie wasn't sure.

"Harry is a great-looking guy," Alice went on. "Minus the drink, he can even be rather charming."

"Unfortunately, the charming part was absent tonight," Annie said.

"Robert's doing well on his program but just can't convince his son Harry to go. It's too bad."

Annie was silent. Her own family had gone through much pain and loss, but not this kind of trauma. She guessed everyone had their own battle to fight.

"You know," Alice said, "talking about the Stevens clan makes me think of something. Harry's grandfather is probably around the same age as your grandmother. Possibly older. I wonder . . ." She drifted off, as if trying to put her thoughts in order.

"I see where this is going," Annie said, excited. "Maybe we can talk to him and find out if he knows anything about those World War II medals."

"Surely we can get some new information," Alice said. "As long as his memory is still good. He's got to be in his late eighties. Or maybe nineties."

"Let's think positive. And we need to remember to show him the photos I found, too. Wouldn't it be great if he could identify the couple? Or even the man?"

"That would be a big help," Alice said, taking a leafy bite of salad.

"Wait a minute." Annie frowned. "I'd probably have to go through Harry to get to his grandfather, wouldn't I?"

"Yes, I expect so."

"Well, that makes me uneasy," Annie said. "I wouldn't want to talk to him about anything."

"I see your point." Alice lapsed into silence and then brightened. "But what about Kate? I bet she can introduce us to Grandpa Stevens just as easily as Harry can."

"After the look Kate just gave me, I don't think I'd be comfortable approaching her. Or any of the Stevens family," Annie said, her expression anxious.

Alice nodded and took another bite of salad, maybe thinking over their options.

As Annie gazed out to the harbor, pondering Kate's glare, their waiter appeared next to the table and set down plates of steaming seafood.

"Pepper?" Derek positioned the pepper grinder over Annie's dish. She gave a polite shake of her head. "No, thanks." That look from Kate had been more hurtful than

Annie realized at first. She felt her stomach knot and looked at her dinner with distaste.

Alice reached across the table and patted Annie's arm. "Let's not allow anything to ruin our lovely meal. Next time you're in A Stitch in Time, she'll be back to normal."

The suggestion of a smile passed over Annie's face. "I hope you're right."

*　　*　　*　　*

Thursday morning it occurred to Annie that the community center auction was only two days away. Yesterday's forays into finding information, plus the delightful dinner with Alice, left no time to work on her afghan project. If she wanted to finish up before the auction, she would have to commit to conversing with her crochet hook. All day.

And maybe tomorrow, as well.

But first Annie hurried into her kitchen to see Wally's progress. He'd still been working when she rushed home and dressed for dinner last night. She couldn't really assess her impressions while dashing out the door. Or in the dim evening light. In fact, lighting was lacking all over the house. She would have to address the issue with Wally. Might as well solve everything at once. At least the problems she knew about.

Annie threw open the windows and back door, letting the scent of the sea chase away the primer's strong smell. Then she stood back and crossed her arms, taking in the untidy scene. Wally had certainly been hard at work.

The old tile counters had been removed, leaving a

distressed wooden surface behind. Annie knew her handyman planned to prep the area before laying the prefabricated granite countertop. And in the typical Wally style, he'd spruced up the room at the end of his workday. Annie appreciated his habits, this one in particular. She could almost make a sandwich on the marred wood, if she didn't mind a splinter or two for garnish.

Cabinet doors were also missing. Each probably stripped and sanded and stored in Wally's own garage waiting for her final verdict. Would she have him stain the cabinets a deep walnut? Or paint them a wonderful color? Annie liked the idea of reusing the functional cupboards, modernizing them with one of the two techniques. But which one?

She sighed. Yet another decision.

Amid the mayhem, she saw walls newly painted with primer, ready for a coat of Jersey Cream. All the old nail holes were gone. The tiny cracks filled. Just a smooth surface for the paint Wally would apply with his artistic touch.

Which reminded her, he would be here soon. Better get moving. Annie filled the kettle and turned up the flame. She pulled the cat food from the shelf and turned to pour some into Boots' bowl. The cat was already sitting beside her dish, waiting. Annie patted her furry head and doled out a generous portion.

"So what do you think, Miss Boots? Do you like the walls? Are you ready for a change?" Annie watched for a response.

But Boots couldn't be bothered. She seemed quite

focused on her feline fare, thank-you-very-much. Her tail twitched as she leaned into her task. She'd probably be occupied for some time, so Annie left her to it.

After making toast and skimming raspberry jam on top, she sat at the farm table and breakfasted. Sipping her tea, Annie reread a letter she had received yesterday from LeeAnn. It made her miss her daughter more than ever. The note was full of reports on the twins' latest activities, an overview of LeeAnn's own interests, plus news of Annie's long-cherished friends. She felt the tug of Texas again, even while she was in the middle of this exciting remodeling project at Grey Gables.

To tempt her mother back to Brookfield, LeeAnn had included drawings the twins created in Sunday school. Annie had barely glanced at them last night before falling into bed, exhausted. Now she spread them out like ancient masterpieces, smoothing the wrinkles with care.

The first was John's rendition of a boat, fishermen lugging in a huge catch. Across the top, it said "I will make you fishers of men." Annie recalled when Wayne had taken John on that first fishing excursion. A rare occurrence because he was always so busy at the dealership. They'd made a great memory that day. She visualized the photos of their beaming grandson, holding high his prize minnow. It only made Annie's heart ache with longing. Both for little John and for Wayne.

Always for Wayne.

Joanna's creation consisted of the words "God loves us" spelled out in large letters, but the letter O in God was a smiling sun radiating out across the page. At the bottom were lots of brightly colored flowers, with butter-flies dancing between the blooms. How precious was that? Tears flooded Annie's eyes and she let them fall.

When she'd wiped away the last of them, she deter-mined to frame the drawings and hang them right in the kitchen where she could see them every day. Every hour if she wanted. It wasn't like having her grandchildren with her, of course. But for now, she could find comfort in even the smallest connection.

Annie added the purchase of matting and frames to her mental to-do list for next time she ventured into town. Probably not today, with the crochet project looming. But soon.

She rinsed off her breakfast things, dabbing some detergent on a brush and giving them an energetic scrub. After returning her clean cup and silverware to their places—an attempt to create calm amid confusion—Annie headed to the living room with Boots following. Grabbing her tote bag, Annie carried it outside to the front porch, a place that always soothed her.

But today, even with a purring Boots curled up on her feet, Annie's thoughts were in a whirl. Paint the cup-boards or stain them? Red appliances or black? Grandpa's medals or someone else's? Approach Harold Stevens on her own or ask Harry? Ask Kate? Stay in Stony Point or return to Texas?

Bent over her project and crocheting like a madwoman, Annie added an inch to her afghan as the morning flew by. Her goal, of course, was to deliver a completed donation by Friday. But her feverish intensity was driven by more than a time pressure. With every stitch, Annie also worked through her hurt from Kate's affront.

Why had she behaved that way? And why to Annie? How should she handle it?

By the time Wally's pickup pulled into her driveway, Annie had a plan.

~ 11 ~

As Annie pointed the Malibu toward Stony Point, she was tempted to leave the window down. But the effect on her just-combed hair was a bit punishing as strands sliced at her face. So she rolled the window up and smoothed wayward wisps behind her pearl earrings.

Today she determined to seek an answer to Kate's strange behavior. She would simply go see her and ask why. Face to face. Kate didn't know her all that well, and it troubled Annie to think she might have hurt her. Knowing this would be resolved today put her in a cheerful mood.

She'd left Wally stirring a bucket of Jersey Cream paint. To Annie, the liquid looked like melted lemon sherbet. Delicious. A good word to define a kitchen. When she returned from town, the walls would be creamy yellow. And almost edible.

These reflections were making her hungry. Turning the car onto Maple Street, Annie considered a visit to the Cup and Saucer. So what if she'd already eaten several meals out this week? Her kitchen was being renovated. She couldn't be expected to cook, could she? Anyway, wasn't it her duty to help support the Stony Point economy?

But first Annie had an appointment with Mayor Butler. He didn't know it yet. But Ian had said to drop by his office at her convenience, and, well, now was a convenient time. For her. She had placed the carved case containing the World War II medals on the back seat. To that, she added the envelope of photos. All of the memorabilia sat atop Grandpa's military file, tossed there yesterday after her meeting with the mayor.

Turning onto Main Street, Annie passed by Magruder's Groceries and Malone's Hardware on the right, the yarn shop and café on the left. She made a right on Oak Lane and steered the car into a parking spot outside of town hall. She checked her reflection in the rearview mirror, deciding it was passable, and got out of the car.

There was no need to take her grandfather's file to Ian's office; he'd already examined it yesterday. Gathering the medals and photo-filled envelope, Annie stepped onto the sidewalk, taking confident strides up the stairs and beneath the town hall's stately façade. She pushed through the double glass doors and walked down the hall to the mayor's office.

Inside, a middle-aged woman with short, silver hair sat behind a reception desk, typing on a keyboard. Annie could find only one flaw with the secretary's image: the microphone/receiver device attached to her ear. It looked as if it grew from her head. Like a cyborg in a science-fiction film. Annie tried not to stare. When had handheld phones gone out of fashion? If Wayne were here, he would have jotted down the gadget's make and model. In truth, she was surprised he hadn't geared her up with one that last year they worked together at the dealership.

The woman stopped typing and looked up with a

pleasant smile. "May I help you?"

A nameplate sat on the desk. Annie read aloud, "Mrs. Charlotte Nash?"

"That's me. I'm Mayor Butler's secretary." She glanced back at the screen. "Do you have an appointment?"

"An informal one," Annie said. "The mayor told me to drop by at my convenience. I'm Annie Dawson."

"Of course. You're Betsy's granddaughter." Mrs. Nash's tone took on more warmth. "We all loved your grandmother. Something of a star around here, you know. I'm so sorry for your loss."

Annie nodded, moved by the words.

"I hate to be the bearer of bad news, but the mayor is out all day. A statewide mayoral meeting." Mrs. Nash checked her computer screen again. "Oh, dear. He has commitments all day tomorrow, too, though I might be able to fit you in between appointments."

"Thanks, anyway. Tomorrow won't work for me." Annie thought of the afghan she'd brought along today, in case she ended up crocheting at A Stitch in Time. She hoped to deliver it by tomorrow. If not, she still needed to take the old Wallace Nutting print and baby afghan over to the auction. "May I leave a message?"

"Of course." Mrs. Nash poised her fingers over the keyboard again. "What is it?"

"Well—" Annie found herself slightly taken aback that the secretary didn't seem concerned about privacy. "Can I just write out a message?"

"Why, of course you may!" Mrs. Nash dug in her top drawer and handed Annie a tablet. She gestured toward a bejeweled cup full of pens and pencils. "Please help yourself."

Annie set the medals case and photos on a nearby chair. The secretary seemed to study the items with interest. Annie laid her purse on top of the case, chose a purple ball-point pen, and wrote out her message:

> Mr. Mayor:
> Dropped by to show you the medals—

She stopped writing and cut her eyes to Mrs. Nash for a moment. The woman was watching, her curiosity showing. Annie crumpled the note and took a clean sheet.

> Mr. Mayor:
> Dropped by to show you the items we discussed yesterday. Sorry to have missed you. But I'm very interested in getting your opinion, so can we set up a time to talk soon? Hope your meeting was productive.
> Kind regards,
> Annie Dawson

"Would you see that Mayor Butler gets this, please?" Annie asked, tearing the page from the tablet, folding it in half, and giving it to the secretary. "I'd appreciate it."

"Of course. I'll add it to his other messages right now."

Annie picked up her things and moved toward the door, turning back to smile her thanks before she left.

Mrs. Charlotte Nash didn't see the smile, because she

was busy typing Annie's message into the computer.

"So much for handwritten notes," muttered Annie as she exited the town hall.

Disappointed she hadn't been able to show the items to Ian, she returned the medals and pictures to the back seat of the car. She grabbed her tote before closing the car door. Her next destination? A Stitch in Time. To have a one-on-one chat with Kate. If Annie had done something to offend, she wanted to make it right. Right now.

Besides, she really needed more of the brick red wool. If she got too much, Annie could use the extra to make a miniature blanket for little Joanna. A Christmas present to wrap herself in Grandma's afghan love. And she could choose some big-boy colors and make one for John, too.

She slung the tote over her shoulder and started for the shop. Along the way, she made a quick decision to visit Finer Things first. They might have a couple of frames she could use for John and Joanna's drawings. Annie ducked into the store, stopping at a display of pricey stainless-steel cookware. Wouldn't that be nice to have in a newly renovated kitchen?

Picking up a gleaming saucepan, she turned it from side to side, catching the light in the shiny finish. Sturdy, stunning, and very heavy. Cookware to last a lifetime. On the other hand, one day in the future when Annie was feeling feeble, closer to the end of her own life, it might be too heavy. What if she dropped her morning eggs, pan and all? She didn't like the visual and set the saucepan back.

Against one wall, picture frames lined the shelves in all sizes and styles. She let her tote fall to the carpet and inspected them one by one: ebony black-lacquered, wood-grained, ceramic, jeweled, silver or brass, ornate, and plain. Beautiful to be sure, but nothing right for the priceless artwork she wanted to highlight.

"Are you finding everything all right?" A thirty-something saleswoman suddenly appeared.

"I was just looking at these frames. Do you have matting, too?"

"No, sorry. Try Malone's. Mike often stocks extra items that enhance our housewares. I think he even has a small art supply section."

Surprised, Annie said, "I never thought of Malone's. But I'll stop by and see." She moved to leave, taking care to dodge the crystal glasses with her tote bag.

Back outside, she stopped, squinted, and plowed through her purse for sunglasses. She slipped them on and, taking a deep breath, trekked toward A Stitch in Time.

"Hi, ladies," she said brightly, removing her glasses.

Kate stood at one end of the counter, putting sale tags on skeins of ribbon yarn. She immediately looked down and studied a multicolored skein, turning it over in her hand.

"Mary Beth, may I talk to you, please?" she said, still pondering the yarn.

"Sure." The shop owner turned, saw Annie, and hurried to the counter. "Sorry, Kate, I forgot to relieve you. Go ahead now." Mary Beth picked up the labeler and, moving into the place just vacated by Kate, began sticking tags on the yarn.

Kate sped from the shop.

"But. . .where did she go?" Annie asked, stunned. "I wanted to talk to her."

"She had an errand," Mary Beth said without looking up. The click of the labeler pierced the silence in the store.

Annie realized the shop was empty. Without the customers or occasional Hook and Needlers stitching and chatting in the circle, the store seemed to have lost its charm.

"Where is everybody?" Annie asked, trying to smile in spite of her discomfort.

Mary Beth looked at Annie, giving her a hard stare. "I'm here. Do you need help finding anything? Yarn? Crochet hooks?" As if this was Annie's first visit to A Stitch in Time. Only without the usual welcome and warmth.

What was happening? Only two days ago, she'd been overwhelmed with the feeling of belonging, of finding a place inside a circle of friends. Now she was on the outside. And she didn't know why.

"No. . .no. I'm fine," Annie said, not feeling fine at all. She thought of the yarn she planned to buy to complete her afghan. "I've got everything I need."

Her face flushed. She longed to leave. Immediately.

"Thanks, anyway, Mary Beth. I'll just catch Kate another time," Annie said, attempting to use a normal voice. She turned toward the door, adjusting her tote bag, feeling foolish for even bringing it into the store.

She almost ran next door to the Cup and Saucer.

The noise and activity inside the diner was a relief. Annie found a booth and sank down, tossing the tote to the side. Familiar, enticing aromas filled the room and reminded her she was hungry. Her eyes searched for Peggy and spotted her serving a family nearby. Annie listened as the chatty waitress told a little booster-seated boy that if he ate both halves of his grilled-cheese sandwich, he could run faster tomorrow. Maybe win a race with his older brother. The boy grinned and took a big bite.

Annie waved her hand as Peggy rushed to another table. Soon the Cup and Saucer seemed a flurry of Peggy-in-pink, zipping past with another tray full of food or hurrying between tables to take more customer orders. But never stopping at Annie's table.

Maybe she should grab that unoccupied stool at the counter? Taking a whole table for herself might be considered bad manners. Especially when lunch-rush seating was at a premium. She didn't want to annoy anyone.

Just as Annie began to gather her things, Lisa, another waitress uniformed in pink, appeared. "What'll you have?" She flipped open her pad to a clean page.

"Well, let's see," Annie said, stalling. She wanted to talk to Peggy about Kate. But she was faced with Lisa instead.

"I haven't had a chance to look at the menu yet," Annie said, spreading out her hands. It was true. Technically. She'd been straining to make eye contact with Peggy.

Lisa raised one eyebrow in disbelief. Then closed the pad with a snap. "I'll come back." She whirled around and crossed the room to take orders from a couple of rough-looking characters with wild hair and unshaven faces.

Had she just been ignored again? Annie frowned.

Granted, today's rush was a frenzy, but not even a fast greeting as her friend passed the table? Had Peggy told Lisa to come in her stead? If so, she hadn't been much more cordial than Peggy.

Which was not cordial at all.

Apparently the shunning that started last night with Kate extended to the yarn shop and now the diner. She couldn't bear staying a moment more and, head down, left the table. The cowbell chimed cheerily as she slunk out. She could feel folks following her exit with their eyes. Annie couldn't dismiss the feeling that everyone knew something. . .except her.

And she was wandering around in the dark.

Alone.

~ 12 ~

When Annie arrived home, she noted Wally outside hunched over his trays and rollers, hosing Jersey Cream paint from a brush. Considering what occurred this afternoon at A Stitch in Time and the Cup and Saucer, she almost expected her handyman to throw down the hose in disgust when he saw her, turn, and stomp out of sight.

Instead, he shot a playful spray of water her way and waved the wet brush. "Hey, Mrs. D., check out the kitchen." Wally nodded toward the porch, urging Annie inside the house for a look.

She took the porch steps with a lightness borne of relief. Would he still be as warm tomorrow after a talk with Peggy? Annie pushed the thought away. She had enough troubles without looking for more.

The cat waited inside the front door to weave herself around Annie's ankles. Reaching down to scratch Boots' back, her mistress mused how nice that she'd received such a spirited welcome, even if it was only from a stray kitty.

"Come on, Miss Boots. You deserve a treat." Annie untangled her feet from the cat and took a few steps. With a meow that sounded annoyed, the cat trotted ahead toward the kitchen. By the time Annie caught up, Boots was standing guard beside her dish.

Taking in Wally's work, Annie caught her breath, delighted. The walls glowed with a soft yellow, the color of fresh-shucked corn. She imagined how the completed kitchen might look with the new backsplash, updated cupboards, hardware, black granite countertops, and, of course, her red Victorian-style appliances. Or black.

"So, what do you think?" Wally's voice resonated as he came alongside.

There was pride in his tone. And well earned, by Annie's high standard.

"Gram would love it, Wally, and so do I," she said, looking around with admiration. "Even though we're at the beginning of this project, I've seen the quality of your work on the outside of Grey Gables. And you did a beautiful job on the living room, too. So I know it will be stunning when this room is done."

"Thanks," he said, running his fingers through shaggy brown hair. "Once that paint sets, I'll sand the cupboards. Then you really need to tell me what you want. Paint or stain."

"I can't decide." Annie bit her lower lip. "I just don't want to do anything Gram wouldn't approve of, you know?" Though Gram would probably encourage her to take a risk and want Annie to please herself.

Wally frowned. "Here's the problem. I have to do more prep work if you want the cabinets stained. If you want them painted, it won't take as long."

"That makes sense."

"Less time, less money, too."

Annie wasn't so worried about the extra money,

though maybe she should be. These projects had a way of wrestling cash from one's pocketbook without a fight. The expense of Victorian-style appliances would push this remodel into new financial territory. That was a fact. She made an on-the-spot decision.

"Let's paint them."

"Paint it is." Wally walked over to a windowsill and pulled off a fragment of painter's tape he'd missed in cleanup. "Got a color in mind?"

Oh, no. She wasn't sure. "Not really."

"May I make a suggestion?"

"Yes, please do!" Annie appreciated the expertise. He'd probably seen many combinations of color and paint in his work.

"I like that white you chose for trim. What about that?"

"Well," she said with hesitation, "white's okay. But that's a high gloss."

Wally nodded. "Exactly. I can get more, no problem. Your account at Malone's is still good, right?"

Annie smiled. "Right."

"Here's what I'm thinking," Wally said. "The white will lighten up your space and look crisp with the new black counters. It will showcase your grandmother's collectibles and the gloss will give a modern, edgy feel."

"You make a good point. Or several good ones," Annie said. "I like the way you think, Wally. White will work well."

"And, if you want, I could cut the middle out of this row of cupboards and replace it with glass." He ambled back over and stood next to Annie, leaning toward her. "Then all these fine old heirlooms could be on permanent display."

"That's true," Annie agreed. And she'd have to make sure the cupboards were always neat and clean. That could be a drawback. Or a blessing. Overall, the plan was an inexpensive fix that would change the complexion of the kitchen for the better.

She approved. "Let's do it!"

After Wally left, Annie's mood moved from excited to exhausted, in spite of the wonders of her new kitchen. She sank down onto a hard chair at the table and massaged her brow, feeling a bit woozy. Should she eat something? Annie recalled her embarrassing afternoon exodus out of the Cup and Saucer. Without lunch.

She should be hungry. But she wasn't, though her hands trembled a little. Maybe a little nap? Or was that a little escape? Everything seemed to make her emotional. Since Wayne's death, she'd turned more tender, which was the way Annie liked to put it. As if she could feel things more deeply. The losses. . .the loneliness. . .the trials of life.

The snubs of friends.

Boots gave a feline whine and stretched. She'd given Annie enough time.

"Okay, okay. I owe you some cat food. It's coming." Annie struggled to her feet, fatigue washing over her. She fed the cat and then opened the refrigerator door, looking for a snack. A Styrofoam container housed the remains of last night's garlic shrimp. She pulled it out, thinking of a treat for Boots, but changed her mind. Loud chomping noises confirmed that the cat was content.

Annie grabbed a bag of loose lettuce and, instead, fashioned a shrimp salad for herself. Too tired to make a dressing, she added a handful of crackers to her meal. Sitting back down, she ate slowly, again pondering the behavior of the women.

They were friends, weren't they?

She must have said or done something wrong. What other explanation was there?

The answer was more of a mystery than Annie had ever faced.

If Wayne were here, he'd tell her to confront her problem head on. "Don't wait for things to get out of hand. Tackle your troubles right away. Or they'll grow so big in your imagination you'll be powerless to overcome them." He was right, of course.

But wasn't that what she'd tried to do today?

She needed some good advice. But from whom? Who was still talking to her besides Wally? And he might not be so affable tomorrow. How would she deal with that little challenge?

Sighing, she cleared away her late lunch and put the kettle on. While she waited for water to boil, she determined to call Alice. No one could better assess the situation than her neighbor and friend who was a Stony Point native.

If they were still on speaking terms.

Annie took her tea into the living room, sat on the sofa and, firming her resolve, dialed Alice's number.

"I was just thinking about you," Alice said. "About last night and especially about Kate's strange behavior."

"It's gotten worse," Annie said, thankful to hear the acceptance in her friend's voice. "Let me tell you what happened today." She poured out the afternoon's upsetting experience.

"Put the kettle on," Alice said. "I'll be right over."

The water was still steaming when Alice stepped inside the house. Annie gave her a grateful hug, and they headed toward the kitchen. Alice plunked herself into one of the green chairs, setting a basket in the center of the farm table. She pulled away the linen towel, cross-stitched with pumpkins and winding vines of green leaves, reminiscent of Cinderella's magic coach. Alice's handiwork, no doubt.

"Pumpkin nut bread. Hot out of the oven." Alice pushed the basket toward Annie, who had placed a cup of steaming hot water and a teabag in front of her. "With matching linen, no less."

"It's beautiful work, Alice. And the bread." Annie breathed in the spicy aroma. "It smells wonderful! But isn't it a little early for pumpkins?"

Alice shook her head. "In my book, it's never too early for pumpkins. Besides, waiting all year for Thanksgiving makes my pumpkin passion grow so unbearably strong that by the time the season actually arrives, I'm in a state of starvation. Pumpkin bread, pumpkin cookies, pumpkin scones—I inhale it all." She helped herself to a plump pumpkin slice. "I gained five pounds last fall."

Annie laughed. Having Alice here returned everything to normal. Even Annie's energy returned. "Don't be so hard on yourself. After all, it *is* a vegetable, right?"

Alice stopped. "Why didn't I think of that before? It changes everything. Now I can eat this vegetable guilt-free." She sank her teeth into the pumpkin nut bread again.

After they had shared several slices between them, Annie asked, "What do you think is going on with Kate? And not only her, but Mary Beth and Peggy. Peggy saw me, I know. But she didn't even acknowledge me or come by the table." Annie shrugged. "That just doesn't seem like Peggy to me."

"I agree. Peggy likes to chat. And she really admires you, Annie." Alice used her fingertip to pick up the last pumpkin crumbs on her plate. "This is a puzzle for sure."

Annie grew thoughtful. "I don't know what to do. It's all so bizarre, I was even worried maybe you and I weren't speaking anymore."

Alice stopped her nibbling. "Don't you ever, ever think that again. We have been friends since we were children and always will be. And if you move back to Texas, we won't allow the miles to come between us. No getting rid of me, I'm afraid."

"Good. That's how I feel, too, Alice. Amid all the loss of the last year or so, I've been given a great gift. That's you and our friendship."

Alice blinked rapidly. She patted Annie's hand, in an apparent attempt to comfort. "Let me make a couple of calls and see what I can find out."

"Would you? I'd be so grateful, though I don't want to come between you and the others."

"Don't worry about that." She covered the basket of bread and pushed it away. Surveying the kitchen, she said, "I like what you're doing with the place."

Thankful for a change of subject, Annie said, "You like the yellow?"

"Love it."

"Wally's going to paint the cupboards a glossy white." Annie explained the decisions she had made so far. "I wonder if Gram would approve of my choices in here."

"Annie, remember that sampler Betsy made for me? It says, 'To everything there is a season. A time for every purpose under heaven.' Now is your time to make the decisions for Grey Gables. Betsy left the house to you, her only and most beloved grandchild. I know she would approve of your making it your own, Annie. It's your season, after all."

Annie nodded. "Thank you for saying that. But, as I recall, that sampler also says to keep your heart open for love—or something. What do we do with that statement?"

"It actually says, 'Keep your head held high and your heart ready for love.' I think you should take the first part under advisement. You haven't done anything wrong so far as I can see. The second part? The having your heart ready for love part? Well," Alice hesitated and then said, "Good luck with that."

⁓ 13 ⁓

The next morning was Friday, the deadline for all auction items to be dropped off at the Stony Point Community Church. Annie had tried to finish up her afghan the night before but had run completely out of the brick red yarn. Perhaps the afghan was destined for the missionary cupboard back in her Brookfield church.

She put together a box containing both baby afghans she'd made, along with the Wallace Nutting print, sandwiching it between the soft coverlets for safe transport. It didn't seem like much. Not for Betsy Holden's granddaughter, anyway. Gram would have given more.

Annie searched among the living room's treasures for something else. She touched a Tiffany-style lamp with its intricate stained-glass pattern. No, not that. She used it every evening. Besides, she remembered watching Gram stitch in its soft light. What about the little figurine on the end table? Not that one either. It was a gift from Grandpa.

Finally she picked up a favorite pillow with a cross-stitched harbor scene in the center. Another Betsy Original. It would bring a great deal more than any of the items she had selected. She put it in the box and took a few deep breaths. Could she give up something so special of Gram's? Something she had created by hand? Even for charity? Steeling herself, she taped the box closed and wrote a description of the items inside for whoever would set up the auction list. Before she could change her mind, she carted the container out to the car and loaded it into the trunk. Out of her sight.

Returning to the living room for her purse, Annie felt the loss of the pillow. Or was it the loss of Betsy's presence? That was ridiculous. The entire house shouted Betsy's name to anyone who entered.

Don't be so selfish.

Annie hurried to the Malibu, climbed in, started the engine, and turned down Ocean Drive. It was the usual scenic route, but she hardly noticed the view. Her brain was too active attempting to solve the mysteries of Kate and the medals.

She had maneuvered her vehicle into a parking space in the crowded church lot before she realized it. Wrestling the box from the trunk, she carried it up the walk. The white clapboard building was typical New England fare, served up with gracious trees and generous lawns. Not fancy in the style of some structures, but the requisite steeple placed it fully into quaint category. Annie had often thought it would make a charming scene in a snow globe.

She entered the small sanctuary, passing rows of wooden pews lit by chandeliers, and walked through a side door. Finding herself in a hallway, Annie headed toward the door that opened into the big church kitchen. Inside was a hub of activity as industrious as Santa's workshop. And everywhere, tables were covered with all manner of donations. Rather like Gram's attic.

A couple of men were carrying furniture out into the hall and across into an open Sunday school room. Between two busy volunteers, she saw Gwendolyn Palmer, writing on a pad and taping numbers to several items culled from the rest. With a little sigh of gratitude, Annie made her way between people and boxes until she was in front of Gwendolyn.

Annie squeezed her box between a couple of others at Gwendolyn's table. "You sure look busy, Gwendolyn. Need any help?"

"This is the biggest event we've ever had. We sure could use more . . ." Gwendolyn looked up and stopped abruptly. "Oh."

Annie pushed the box toward Gwendolyn. "I just brought this stuff down for the auction. Maybe it will bring in something for the fund."

"Thank you. I'll just catalog this and give you a receipt so you can get on your way." Gwendolyn cut through the tape and opened the flaps. She lifted out the pillow, drawing in a breath, her eyes wide. "Annie! This is Betsy's work, isn't it? I'd know that exquisite stitching anywhere."

"Yes," Annie said, pleased at the reaction. "I'll admit it's hard to give up. But I know Gram would have given even more. She had a great heart for others."

"That she did." Gwendolyn said, her eyes misting. She set the pillow to the side and pulled out the first baby afghan. "Beautiful work. I'm sure it will draw some bids."

"Thanks."

"And what's this?" Out came the old tinted photo, the glass gleaming inside the frame. "Remember when you used to find these at yard sales for ten dollars?" Gwendolyn shook her head. "Now they can cost hundreds. Why didn't I store up the ten-dollar-types back then for a rainy day?"

"Well, it's not raining out," Annie said. "But I hope this will help put a new roof on the building before it does rain again."

Gwendolyn peered into the box and drew out the second afghan. Raising her eyes to meet Annie's, she said, "So you donated your Texas-bound baby afghan, too. It reminds me of something your grandmother might do." She put the soft cotton yarn next to her cheek. "This one is my favorite. I might have to bid on it."

She added the items to her list and assigned them numbers. Once she'd written out a receipt, Gwendolyn pressed it into Annie's hand and said, "Talk to Kate. You two need to discuss things."

"But. . .what do we have to discuss?" Annie asked, her tone pleading.

"Alice gave me a call this morning, but I told her the problem is between you and Kate."

"But, what have you heard? Please tell me!"

"I'm too busy to get involved," Gwendolyn said. "Just talk to Kate."

"Okay." Annie nodded. How does that happen when Kate won't talk to her? She moved away, feigning interest in the other auction items as she entered the hall. Stepping aside as a man rolled a dolly past, she hurried from the hustle.

Back in the sanctuary, she noticed Reverend Wallace sitting alone in a pew near the back. Annie hated to disrupt his reading but, feeling desperate, she slipped in beside him. "Reverend Wallace? Could I have a word with you?"

He closed his book and gave her a grin. "Good to see you, Mrs. Dawson. How about a walk outside? We can talk there without being interrupted. Too much traffic here."

As he spoke, a couple wandered through with paper bags bursting with something. Probably auction items. "See what I mean?" he said, rising.

They followed a worn path beneath the trees, apparently a favored walk. Annie appreciated the amble under the leafy canopy, shafts of sunlight piercing the shade like laser beams. The serenity of the scene was as welcome as his kindness.

Eventually, they stopped at a picnic table. "If you don't mind, I need to rest this old hip of mine. One day, I suppose I'll need to get it taken care of through surgery, but I'm putting it off as long as I can." He brushed a few leaves off the bench before making himself comfortable, and then he placed the worn book he'd brought with him on the table.

As Annie sat down on one side, she gazed at the older man. Spectacled, with receding gray hair and a gentle manner, he filled her job description of a country parson.

"This is a beautiful spot, Reverend Wallace. I didn't even know it was here," Annie said, stalling a little, not sure how to begin.

He glanced around. "Isn't it? My wife and I often picnic here in the middle of the day. She makes the best chicken salad sandwiches and brownies. I always look forward to her company. But I have to say it is enhanced by her cooking."

"That sounds wonderful," Annie said, smiling. "You're a lucky man."

"Mighty blessed, for sure," the Reverend said. "But you didn't seek me out to hear about my wife's cooking. How can I help you, Mrs. Dawson?"

"Well," she looked down at her hands. Though she wanted his advice, it was awkward, if not embarrassing. "I have a problem."

"I gathered as much," he said. "Take your time. I'm listening."

She might as well get it over. Attack it head on, as Wayne would say. "I seem to have offended a friend without realizing it, and now I feel shunned by her and everyone in our circle. Well, not everyone because my best friend still supports me, but I'm hurt by everyone else's treatment and not sure what to do!" The words poured forth like a verbal tsunami.

Reverend Wallace didn't seem that surprised. "Can you think of anything you might have done or said to get such a reaction? Maybe even a joke gone wrong?"

"No, I really can't," Annie said, her expression baffled. "I've tried to understand, but it's a mystery. At least it is to me, though Kate must have her reasons." She caught her breath. "I didn't mean to mention names. Sorry."

"It won't change my opinion of anyone, even if I know the name. We all have faults, all have shortcomings." He fixed his kind eyes on Annie. "Have you confronted your friend? Tried to talk it out between the two of you?"

Annie sighed. "I did try. But she wouldn't talk to me. When she saw me, she just left. Since then, pretty much all of our friends are siding with her. But about what, I don't know."

"I see." He thought a moment and then spoke. "Here's what I recommend, Mrs. Dawson. Just try and isolate each of your friends and talk to her alone. It's not helpful to have the herd against you, not that I'm calling them a herd, you understand. Let's say instead, it's not good to have a group ganging up against you."

"Okay." She almost grinned. "That makes sense. But what would I say?"

"Approach each one individually and say that you have felt a sudden distance between you. And you are bothered by that. Which you are, of course."

"Yes," Annie said. "I really care about them."

"Then say that, too. That you care and value their friendship. You want to clear up this conflict between you. To make things right."

Annie nodded slowly, wishing she'd talked to Reverend Wallace earlier. Before she'd seen Gwendolyn.

"Folks around here can be a little wary of strangers. You have points in your favor because you are Betsy Holden's granddaughter, but that only goes so far if they think you have hurt one of their own, which is what it sounds like to me." The old gentleman reached over and opened the book, a hymnal, flipping the pages as he spoke. "The main thing is to confront these ladies in love. Love conquers all."

A soft wind rustled the leaves overhead, and Annie thought about all he had said. It wouldn't be easy. She would have to set her pride aside and, as Reverend Wallace advised, approach each one in love.

But how loving did she feel?

"Here it is, one of my favorite hymns," he said. "As we talked, this line came to me: 'Are you weak and heavy-laden, cumbered with a load of care?' And the answer to everything, 'Take it to the Lord in prayer.' " Reverend Wallace closed the book and folded his hands. "May I pray for you, Mrs. Dawson?"

A calm settled over Annie as he prayed. And as they walked back along the path, her spirit at rest, she had a sense that all would be well.

Annie was almost inside her Malibu when she thought of something else. "Reverend Wallace!" she shouted.

"What is it, Mrs. Dawson?" He hurried over to the car. "Is something else bothering you?"

"No, but I wondered if I might ask you one more thing, about someone here in Stony Point."

How much should she share with him? Annie decided to be open. If you couldn't trust a minister, whom could you trust? "I want to talk to Harold Stevens, Harry's grandfather, about a World War II photo that might be of my grandmother in her youth. He probably knew Gram long ago, and I'm hoping he can help identify the people in the picture," Annie said. "But of course, Kate isn't speaking to me."

"Ah, yes. I see. That makes it awkward."

"I'd like to find him myself, but I'm not sure where he is. Any ideas?"

Reverend Wallace nodded, considering. "The last I heard of Harold Stevens, he was moving to an assisted-living facility. But I regret to say I don't recall which one."

He did look full of regret then, perhaps lamenting that he hadn't made a visit to see Harold himself. "Please let me know what you find out."

Annie thanked him and climbed in the car, excited.

Now she had a place to start.

~ 14 ~

After loading up on groceies at Magruder's, checking for frames at Malone's, and having the car washed, Annie was glad to pull into the Grey Gables driveway. Boots met her at the porch's edge, arching her back to meet her mistress's hand and leaning against her pant leg. Annie could always depend on Boots to give her a warm welcome. She scratched along the furry backbone with her free hand and then paused to straighten up and shuffle a bag of groceries to her other hip. That's when Annie saw a white wicker basket resting on the doormat.

Tied to the curved handle was a fluffy yellow bow. Annie thought she knew who it was from. She picked it up and stepped inside the house, holding the door open long enough for Boots to enter. Placing the basket on the coffee table, Annie spotted an envelope. She ripped it open.

Inside was a gift certificate for anything in the Divine Décor catalog. Annie beamed. How thoughtful Alice was. Maybe she would look for something new for the kitchen. She couldn't resist going through the basket right away. It looked as if Alice had been on another cooking kick. More pumpkin bread, some pumpkin scones, and pumpkin spice tartlets. Last, a slim package covered in pumpkin print paper. She unwrapped it with care and opened the box.

"Oh, how lovely!" Annie said aloud. It was a small square cloth cross-stitched with pink roses in each corner. It could serve as a tiny tablecloth for her little moss-rose toy china set. When had Alice stitched up this creation? The workmanship was almost as good as Gram's.

Annie jumped up to call Alice. But before she picked up the phone, she noticed her answering machine flashing furiously, indicating several messages.

She pressed the button. The first was from LeeAnn.

"Mom, is everything okay? Haven't heard from you in a few days. That's not normal, you know!" Annie could hear the worry in her daughter's voice. "Call me. By the way, did you like the drawings the twins made? They're missing you. So am I."

Warmth flooded her heart. She missed them terribly. And that was an understatement. Annie would call them back this evening.

Next was Alice's message, an invitation to dinner tonight. Probably so Annie wouldn't have to cook in her own chaotic kitchen. Alice's neat cottage was always welcoming. And her cross-stitch décor reminded Annie of Gram's style.

A message from Wally followed. "Mrs. D., I'm getting ready to have glass cut for the cupboard doors like we discussed. Here's what I need to know. What kind of glass do you want? It's your call. There's frosted—that would really pump up the modern look. Or patterned glass? Lots of choices—even stained glass. We have some local artisans who could do a good job, but the expense and time . . ." Would the decisions never end? Once she made a final one, it never seemed to be final at all. She was glad the machine cut him off midchoice.

All the messages along with Alice's thoughtful basket were like a tonic for Annie. She decided to return Wally's message first.

What if Peggy answered?

She would simply act as if nothing was wrong.

Maybe Peggy would believe it.

To her good fortune, no one answered at the Carson household. Annie left an upbeat message, telling Wally the plain glass would work fine in the new kitchen. She added that she hoped to see the family at the big auction tomorrow. And took a deep breath in relief.

After carrying in the rest of the groceries, Annie cut herself a slice of Alice's pumpkin bread, plopped down in a kitchen chair, and considered how she might best pursue Harold Stevens. Remembering Reverend Wallace's suggestion, she reached for the telephone book and opened the yellow pages to the listings for assisted-living facilities.

Annie found three listings and wrote them down, along with addresses and telephone numbers. Glancing at her watch, she saw there were still several hours before she was due at Alice's for dinner. Why not do a little sleuthing this afternoon? Annie would have more to share with Alice over dinner. Taking the rest of the pumpkin bread with her, she stuffed the list into her purse and hurried out to the car.

The biggest ad on her list had been for Seaside Hills Assisted Living with an address on Elm Street. Annie thought it might be located near the church and she was right. It was just up the street. Why hadn't Pastor Wallace mentioned that?

She parked out front and approached the wide double doors under a porch overhang. A silver-wigged woman sat in her wheelchair, fingering the strand of beads that lay across her chest. When she saw Annie, her face lit up and she smiled. "Are you here to see me?" the woman asked.

"Well, I certainly am very glad to see you," Annie said, stopping to chat. "I'm Annie Dawson. What's your name?"

"Elizabeth. Elizabeth Taylor," she said. "You've probably seen me in the movies. I was a big star at one time."

She spoke with such assurance that Annie wavered. After all, people do change over time. But this much? She examined the wrinkled face with the liquid brown eyes. It wasn't her. The real Elizabeth Taylor was famed for her violet eyes. Besides, why would she be hidden away in Stony Point when all of Hollywood adored her? Not a chance.

"Nice to meet you, Elizabeth. Are you having a good day?"

Elizabeth shook her finger at Annie. "I said that's all. No more autographs!"

"That's okay. Maybe next time," said Annie, adding, "Those are beautiful beads you're wearing." She moved toward the doors.

"Aren't they? I wore them when I made *Giant* with

Rock Hudson." Elizabeth oozed sweetness again. "Will you be joining us for dinner?"

Declining as politely as possible, Annie stepped inside to the reception desk. A young woman tapped on her computer keyboard. She stopped and faced Annie. "Welcome to Seaside Hills. I'm Tiffany. How may I help you?" It sounded like a well-rehearsed phone salutation that doubled as a face-to-face greeting.

"I hope you can help me, Tiffany," Annie said. "I'm trying to locate Harold Stevens and was told he might be residing here."

She shook her head. "That's Harry Stevens' grand-father, isn't it? Sorry, not here. We had a Harold Warnock for a time. Nice old guy. But that doesn't help, does it?"

Annie didn't want to waste the trip. "Do you have any other folks who have been lifelong residents of Stony Point? Maybe in their late eighties? Or early nineties?"

"Do you have a family member here?" The reception-ist's response became less helpful. Protective.

"Actually, I'm looking for information about my grand-mother, Betsy Holden. She passed away recently, and I'm anxious to find folks who may have known her. Especially if they lived here in the 1940s."

Tiffany seemed to relax. "I see. We do have some lifelong Stony Point residents, but few will be able to speak to you. This is a fairly high-functioning facility, but many residents are unable to remember or even communicate because of one thing or another. Dementia, strokes, and so on."

"I understand," Annie said, disappointed.

"There is someone," Tiffany said. "She's been here all her life, and she's about the right age. You may have passed her when you came in. Her name is Elizabeth."

"Ah, yes, Elizabeth." Annie sighed. "Thanks."

"You must have talked to her already," Tiffany said, a little grin playing over her lips. "Her name really is Elizabeth Taylor. She gets her dreams mixed up with real life sometimes. But if you guide her back to that time, she may have some information for you."

"I'll do that." Maybe Annie would end up with some information after all. She was about to leave when Tiffany spoke again.

"Wait! Why didn't I think of it before? I'll just call his grandson Harry. My husband works on his fishing crew, so I know the number by heart." Tiffany dialed as she spoke. "I'm sure Harry can tell us where his grandfather is staying."

"No, please. Don't go to any trouble." The last thing Annie needed was to make Kate think she was poking around into her family affairs or bothering old Harold Stevens. Not after the angry looks at the restaurant. "I can figure it out."

"No trouble at all," Tiffany said, tapping her nails on the desk until the other party apparently picked up. She asked for Harry and waited again before identifying herself. "Mr. Stevens? Sorry to bother you, but I have someone here who is interested in finding your grandfather, to ask him some questions." She continued to pour out information, including Annie's identity as Betsy Holden's granddaughter.

Annie's shoulders sagged. This couldn't be good. She didn't need another reason for Harry or Kate to be angry with her. Apparently there was already reason enough, though Annie was still in the dark about that mystery, too.

Tiffany ended the call, scribbled some words on a note, and held it out. "Here you go. Harold resides at Ocean View Assisted Living."

Annie took the paper, murmured her thanks, and escaped outside. She just hoped the episode wouldn't create more problems with Kate. Meanwhile, she might as well see if Elizabeth knew anything about Harold or her grandparents. The senior still sat stroking her beads. Several lawn chairs encircled her at different angles. Annie dragged one up next to the woman and took a deep breath.

"Hello, Elizabeth. I just heard that you are a long-time Stony Point resident."

"Oh, yes. Isn't it a beautiful spot? I've lived here all my life, right in this house."

Not a good start. Annie tried again. "Do you remember a man named Harold Stevens? Maybe he was a friend of yours?"

Elizabeth laughed out loud. "A friend of mine? No, he never noticed me, though Harold liked the ladies. He was sweet on that one gal. But I don't remember her name." She looked into the distance, as if reliving that time.

Annie caught her breath. "Was it Betsy? Betsy Holden?"

"Did you know Betsy, too? She was a lovely girl. Married

Charlie. Betsy and Charlie, sitting in a tree, k-i-s-s—"

"Got it," Annie said, pushing back her disappointment, stopping the familiar phrase. She checked her watch, realizing she needed to leave or be late for dinner at Alice's. "Thanks for the visit. Maybe I'll come back and see you again. Would that be okay?"

"That would be nice, dear." Elizabeth's brown eyes shone. "Next time, you'll have to stay for dinner."

"Next time, I will," Annie promised, waving as she headed toward the car. The visit had produced a good haul. She now knew where to find Harold Stevens. Though there wasn't time to visit him today.

But she also might have stirred up the fire with Kate.

Should Annie have come at all?

Still, she had met a movie star. With a clue. Harold Stevens loved the ladies.

But what that meant to the overall picture created another mystery.

~ 15 ~

Saturday morning Annie slid her car into a just vacated spot on the outer edge of the church parking lot. Celebrating such a piece of luck, she stepped out onto the pavement. Now, if her auction items made some decent money for the building fund, especially Gram's pillow, this day would only get better.

Last night's dinner at Alice's had offered Annie an opportunity to tell her friend about running into Gwendolyn at the church earlier and their uneasy interaction.

"I appreciate that you called her." Annie had said. "I'm sure she was more pleasant toward me because of it."

"Good. I called Stella, too. Their loyalties seem to be with Kate, although they won't tell me what the problem is. Of course, they've known her so long."

"And she's a townie."

"You got it." Alice had pondered the problem. "I'll think of something. If only someone would tell us why."

"That would help a lot." Annie went on to relate the kind advice from Reverend Wallace. "I'm not sure how if it will work with Kate, but I do want to speak to each Hook and Needle Club member alone. That seemed like wise counsel to me. Maybe I can find a way to catch one or two of them at the auction."

Annie looped her purse over a shoulder, hoping the

plans they had laid last night would come to fruition today. She walked to the church's side entrance, a direct route into the big community center room. As she neared the door, the mass of humanity narrowed into a single line, merging like cattle into a chute. Along the side of the building hung a banner announcing "Community Auction—11:00 A.M.—until it's all gone!" Because she would be at the church, Annie had dressed with care: black trousers, black flats, and pink pull-over sweater. Staring at the others in line, she seemed overdressed. Most were wearing jeans and sweatshirts. She stuffed her pearl necklace inside the neck of her sweater.

She waited her turn to cross the threshold, trying not to push people or get in anyone's way. Annie recognized a few people. She waved and most returned the greeting. The others must not have seen her. Their mood seemed to match her own—expectant. Would one of the bidders accidentally acquire an undiscovered Vermeer or Picasso?

Though in truth, she never cared much for Picasso. But a Vermeer—

Once she was inside the building, her excitement increased. Annie attempted to remain composed. She noticed numerous rows of folding chairs, the early birds already seated, scrutinizing the list of items soon up for bid. Near the wall, long tables had been set up, laden with diverse items, some boxed, some separate. Over in one corner, ladies from the church served coffee, soda, and snacks. Music blared over the public address system, adding to the festive feel.

The scene reminded her of a country fair. It didn't

match the auction environment of her imagination: price-less treasures, hushed voices, carpeted aisles, and snooty matrons. Wherever had she gotten that idea? Maybe it came from the pages of a Victorian novel.

Annie was eager to get started. The line moved forward a couple of feet. Only three people were ahead of her now. Not knowing the procedure once she reached the front, she started to panic. Where was Alice?

She spotted her friend purchasing a snack at the back table. Annie caught Alice's eye and waved her over. "I was looking for you," Annie said, accepting a lemon bar Alice had bought. "What do I do when I get to the front of the line?"

"Obviously, you've never attended a Stony Point auction! It's a pretty relaxed event. I'll help you get your bearings. First, we'll sign you up and get your paddle. I'm lucky number 15," Alice said, spinning her paddle around to show the number stenciled on one side.

"I thought the lucky number was seven." Annie hid a smile.

"Didn't get here early enough to be that lucky. You'll receive a list of the auction items by lot number. Over there on that table are some of the lots."

"Funny, but some of the lots don't seem to have a lot to them." Annie indicated an item at the end of the nearest table. "Like that clock for instance. Is that a part of a lot?"

Alice glanced where Annie had pointed. "It's a lot all on its own."

"Doesn't look like that much. Certainly not a lot. Well, I see I'll need to adapt to the terms of engagement, so to speak."

"Yes, you will." Alice took several steps forward as the line moved, pulling Annie along. "You're next. Get out your credit card."

When Annie's turn came, she had her credit card in hand, along with identification. The man on the other side of the counter wasn't familiar to her, but he gave her a broad smile anyway. She handed him the plastic card. He scanned it through a machine and waited before handing it back.

"That works. Driver's license, please," he said.

Annie handed it over.

"A Texas transplant, eh?" He handed it back to her, along with a paddle. "Number 29. Good luck to you."

"Thanks." Taking her paddle, Annie grabbed Alice's arm. "Let's go get a good seat before they fill up. Look at that crowd."

They found seats five rows back and along the outside of the area. Prime property, Alice pointed out. Not only were they close enough to get a good view of each item presented for auction, but they could see who bid. "And we'll know what they bid on. That might matter as the bidding progresses."

"Why?" Annie asked.

"You might get in a bidding war over something," Alice said. "Say you wanted that darling little table over there. But the gal in the blue top outbid everyone for any table that came up. You'd know there wasn't much chance for you to win your table if that gal won every bid."

"Why would she bid on *every* table? How many tables would one need?"

"Maybe she needs lots of tables for some reason. She could have just bought a bed and breakfast business and is outfitting all the rooms. Or has a store in a nearby town called Tableworld or something. It doesn't matter. That's not the point."

"What's the point then?"

Alice bent closer, keeping her voice low. "It gives you a kind of power."

"Power? I don't see how."

"If you know she's going to fight you for the table, you can make the decision to give it up, or—" Alice's gaze darted about as if to make sure no one overheard, "you can drive up the bid."

"Drive up the bid? I'm not sure I follow you."

"Well, if you can't have the table you really wanted, at least the one who insists on outbidding you will have to pay a pretty price for it!"

"But that's so mean!" The shock on Annie's face made Alice laugh out loud.

"It is, isn't it? And I've seen it happen once or twice over the years. Not," Alice said, defensively, "that either of us would ever think of doing such a thing."

"Of course not."

"Still, it has its benefits."

"Like what?" Annie asked, wondering how her friend could make a positive spin out of their conversation.

"You'll see. Trust me." Alice's answer remained a mystery.

Annie turned to her list, studying the less-than-helpful descriptions of the lots. Just titles, really.

"How am I supposed to know what's in those boxes or how old things are?"

"We need to preview the auction. See all those folks crowded around the tables? That's what they're doing." Alice scanned the room, looking for something. Or someone. "Annie, I'll be right back."

She jumped up and dashed across to the snack and soda table, disappearing into the folks gathered about the area. Soon she returned, trailed by two teen girls. Alice made the introductions.

"Hannah and Holly, meet Mrs. Dawson. The girls are going to babysit our seats for us while we preview. Isn't that nice?" Alice seemed quite satisfied with the arrangement as they all got acquainted.

"Are you twins?" Annie asked, looking from one to the other. They were so similar.

"People think we are," said Holly, giggling. "But we're not. I think it would be fun."

"You are very alike, I must say." Annie wanted to tell them about her twin grandchildren, but Alice's tapping foot signaled the end of the little gab session. "Thanks for saving our seats."

"Thank you for paying us each ten bucks," Hannah said.

"Don't you love easy money?" Holly added with an expression of delight.

"Ten bu—"Annie started to protest but Alice elbowed her toward the hallway.

"It's a bargain, believe me. Let's preview all the stuff back there first. The bulky items—like chairs and player pianos and whatnot—are in the Sunday school rooms.

You'd be surprised how much they can fit in there. We can check out the boxed lots and little stuff later." Alice sped through the open doorway, stopping just across the threshold to wait for Annie. "Come on, lady-fair. We've got shopping to do."

Once inside the first room, Annie's pulse perked up even more. Rows of merchandise littered the space, reminding her of Gram's attic. She followed Alice to the beginning of the first row, featuring a portable air conditioner, still in its box.

"Must have been purchased by a desert dweller. Not so needed here on the balmy coast of Maine." Alice wandered along the row. "Some of this stuff looks like garage sale specials."

"I'm not impressed." Annie didn't see one tempting thing so far.

Alice paused in front of an ornate wicker chair. "Look at this! Wouldn't it be pretty on your front porch, Annie?"

It was exceptionally attractive and looked sturdy, in spite of its age. "I love it. Maybe I could bid on this one?"

Alice rattled her paper list. "Make a note next to the lot number. Write down comments, or you'll forget if this was the one you wanted when it comes up for auction."

Annie wrote LOVE IT next to lot number 37. She'd found a wonderful treasure in only the first few minutes.

Apparently she wasn't the only one. A couple of previewers jotted down notes as they stood nearby and discussed the merits of the wicker chair. Another woman, the lady in the blue shirt Alice had used as an example of bad bidding, slipped into the mix and started making notes of her own. Annie's fervor fell a notch. Why were these people focusing on her selection? There was a whole roomful of stuff for *them*.

Make that several rooms full.

Alice, the auction expert, disappeared into the hall.

Annie wasn't quite through looking and lingered at the door.

"I found a bunch more," Alice called out from the next room. At the sound of her voice, the whole group of interested previewers moved as one past Annie to the next wicker lot. She followed.

The wicker devotees scribbled on their lists.

Frowning, Annie also made notes next to each lot number. Except for number 31, a charming chair that lost its charm once inspected closely. "Oh, look. A broken leg. Too bad. Otherwise, it's a beauty."

"Pretty hard to overlook a broken leg. Especially when you have all these perfect ones," Alice said.

"True." Annie continued down the rest of the row and around to the next, not making notes on a refrigerator, a couple of floor lamps, an ornate oak armoire, a work bench, several bicycles of questionable age, and a tread-mill in like-new condition. Most of the items seemed shabby and unappealing. "This looks like junk."

"Placed all together it does. But believe me," Alice said, her tone confidential as she pointed to a rocker-recliner, "when you see this chair by itself, you'll suddenly be consumed by the desire to have it. As if you've never seen one more beautiful in your life!"

She chuckled, but not as though it were a joke. Rather, as if it were a depressing fact.

"Hmm." Annie studied the recliner, noncommittal. Alice's premise seemed unlikely at best. She ambled on, indifferent to the allure of the auction items.

Until she joined Alice in front of an antique dresser. "This is the one," Alice said, whispering just loud enough for Annie to hear. "It's perfect. Act like you hate it."

Now it was Annie's turn to laugh. "What are you talking about? This is a lovely piece. You should bid."

Alice walked away and stood in front of another treadmill, checking it over, making notes on her list.

"Are you bidding on this?" Annie asked. "I thought you liked the dresser."

"I do. Just trying to fool the other bidders, so they won't examine it very well." She turned to face Annie. "Wouldn't it make the most beautiful bathroom cabinet? I could have Wally drop a sink in the top and plumb it. I'm in love."

"With Wally or the cabinet?"

"I might end up a little in love with Wally, too, after he finishes the job. Isn't it great? Not too tall, not too wide, perfect legs."

"Many people might say the same of you, my friend." Annie tried to suppress her smile, unsuccessfully.

"Oh, you! Let's get back in there and check out the boxed lots. We've seen enough."

"I know I have," Annie said, leading the way. She rounded the doorway and smacked into someone head on.

It was Kate.

~ 16 ~

"Excuse me, Kate. I'm so sorry! I. . .I . . ." Annie sputtered her apology.

"Never mind." Kate narrowed her eyes. "Please get out of my way."

Annie stepped to the side. Kate stomped around her and into the Sunday school room.

"Well, that was rude," Alice said as she watched Kate march away.

"At least she said please." Annie tried to make light of the situation. Then her expression became pained. "I haven't helped matters at all, have I? Today I planned to try to talk to Kate alone. This friction between us is just awful. I want it to end."

Alice started to speak; then she apparently thought better of it and clamped her lips into a thin line. Instead she guided Annie to the row of tables nearest the community room wall. They walked along, surveying the odd collection of items. An old violin and bow minus the strings, a ham radio, an old dial telephone, a coin collection with some of the coins missing, a box of sheet music from the 1940s, a chain saw in its plastic case, a box of avocado green glasses in different sizes, and a red plastic box with black knobs.

"That's a guitar amplifier," Annie said in response to Alice's blank look.

"I wondered. Actually, I prefer antique auctions. A guitar whatever wouldn't make it into the final floor show." Alice pointed to a box, lifting something out. "Look!"

"Gram's pillow." Annie noted the lot number with a pang, pushing away a longing for it to be back at Grey Gables. Instead, she determined to be sure and pay attention when it came up for bid. Maybe it would make a lot of money and honor Gram's memory in the doing.

Next to Betsy's boxed pillow, Annie found frames. A box of frames in many sizes. She flipped through them, seeing three that looked to be the right size for her grand-children's precious drawings.

"You could paint those," Alice said.

"Exactly what I was thinking. In fact, I could use the same paint as the cabinets. Or do you think that would be too mixy-matchy?"

They were busy debating the issue when a familiar voice interrupted them. "Finding any bargains, ladies?"

"Ian!" Annie said, "I didn't expect to see you today. How was your big meeting?"

"Very productive, to use the wording of your note." Ian gave a slight bow. "I was sorry to have missed your visit, Annie. And a chance to examine those mysterious medals."

"Me, too. I would have liked to get your opinion."

"And I would have liked to give it," he said, smiling. "Can we set up another time to meet and talk about the medals?"

"What about today?" Annie asked. "I never took them out of my car."

Alice, who had been standing by quietly, said, "Annie, today won't work. You have some special plans, remember?"

Annie knew Alice referred to talking with the women in the Hook and Needle Club, especially with Kate.

"Alice is right. I do have some things I need to do. But can we leave it open? The medals are right in the car. Maybe after the auction?"

"Done," the mayor said. "Now if you'll forgive me, I have to talk to a man about a horse. Or maybe that was a house." He grinned and moved in the direction of the auctioneer, stopping to have a few words here and there with folks along the way.

Annie and Alice previewed the final boxes of items in a rush, eager to arm themselves with sodas and snacks before the auction began at eleven. Annie said good-bye to her baby afghans and the Nutting print. Alice stopped to stroke an Autoharp, saying she'd always wanted one, but Annie pulled her away to take their chosen chairs.

From her vantage point, Annie could see everyone, those seated in front, to the side, and some still previewing the boxed lots. If she stood, she could scan the entire room. She found where Stella sat, as well as Mary Beth. Gwendolyn was still heartily volunteering, making change for a couple of teenaged girls who had loaded up on cupcakes and bags of chips.

On second scan, Annie identified them as Hannah and Holly. Apparently, their twenty dollars was headed for the church roof.

Mayor Butler's familiar voice came over the loud-speaker. "Ladies and gentlemen of Stony Point, and honored guests. Welcome to the fifth annual community auction. I want to thank everyone who donated these wonderful items and all our fantastic volunteers. There are no people with bigger hearts than the folks of Stony Point.

"Now let's enjoy ourselves. Know that when you win a bid, you'll not only take home the item you wanted, but you'll buy a plank of new siding or shingles for the roof. Your generosity will help repair Stony Point Community Church, a cherished place of worship that also serves as our community center. We appreciate you all and thank you from the bottom of our hearts. Let the bidding begin!"

The mayor handed the microphone over to the auctioneer with a flourish, as if it were keys to the city. The crowd clapped and whistled as the mayor exited the room with a wave. To the right, Annie saw the air conditioner carried to the front by a couple of men, one of whom she recognized as Mike Malone. It seemed like everyone in town was either here or involved in some way.

"What am I bid for this portable E-Z air conditioner, new in the box? You won't find a deal like this again, folks. Let's start the bidding at twenty-five dollars. Thank you, sir. Do I hear thirty?" Tommy O'Connor, the auctioneer, began to get in his groove. The auction had begun.

Annie watched item after item auctioned off, some for fantastic prices, others going for much less than she would have expected. And Alice had been right. Each item shown by itself seemed less shabby and more desirable than Annie had imagined. When she noticed a teal-green, overstuffed chair up for bid, she tapped Alice's arm.

"Where did that come from? Isn't it beautiful? I wonder where I could put something like that."

"That's the same ugly rocker-recliner we previewed earlier," whispered Alice. "I told you everything looks new when they display it up front. I can't figure it out. It's like magic."

"Oh, right." Annie put her paddle back in her lap.

Several nice dressers were auctioned off before Alice's pick came up for bid. She played it smart, waiting to see the level of interest on the item. It was modest. As the auctioneer began chanting, "Going once, going twice . . ." Alice raised her paddle and added another ten dollars to the bid. She only had to repeat the process one more time before the other bidder decided to drop out and try for a different, more affordable dresser.

"Sold to bidder number 15!" Tommy O'Connor's voice rang out over the PA.

Excited, Annie gave a little clap and turned to Alice. "Congratulations! You got it."

"Thanks," Alice said, apparently choosing to play it cool, again busy checking her list. "I wonder how long we'll have to wait until that Autoharp comes up. Can't you just imagine me zinging my way through 'My Bonnie Lies over the Ocean'?"

"No, I cannot," Annie said. "Look! Is that one of the wicker pieces?" She spun her paddle in a nervous warm-up, ready to win one for the porch. Though it wasn't a sure thing; there seemed to be so much interest in the wicker lot during the preview.

"Good luck, Annie," Alice said. "Remember: hold to your limit. There are lots of pieces. You'll get another chance."

But each time Annie bid, the woman in the blue top thrust her paddle into the air and just held it there until everyone else quit bidding. It didn't seem to matter how high the price went either. When the fifth wicker chair came up for bid, Annie didn't even put up her paddle.

"That woman is a glutton. Who can compete against her?" Annie said, thoroughly frustrated. "I'm not bothering to bid this time."

Tommy's voice announced, "Twenty-five, twenty-five... who will give me twenty-five dollars?"

Alice nudged Annie. "She's not bidding on this one. So you can try for it. Bid!"

"It won't matter if I do; Miss Blue Top will outbid me anyway." Annie put up her paddle.

"Sold! To bidder number 29."

"That's my number. My goodness, I won!" Annie couldn't believe her luck.

"Congratulations. You can have Wally paint it for you. It will be beautiful. Good for you, Annie." Alice beamed like a proud mama.

"I wonder why Blue Top didn't bid."

"Maybe she had all the chairs she needed. She got four; that's a set. Or she got tired of holding up that heavy paddle." Alice was full of suggestions. "Don't worry about it."

But Annie wasn't so sure, and her happy mood began to drain away. She needed some good food, not just snacks. "How long does this go on?" she asked. Since she had won the chair, there was less reason to stay at the auction.

"Don't you want to see what Betsy's pillow will go for? And what about the frames?"

"Won't they come up much later? Couldn't we take a break and go get a late lunch?"

"We'll lose our seats," Alice said. "We might have to stand."

"I feel like standing, actually. Many people are leaving, anyway, now that they've gotten their items of choice." Annie indicated the unfilled seats scattered about.

"Okay. Wait here; I see Peggy. Let me find out if the Cup and Saucer is able to handle all the extra people in town today. If there's a long wait, we might as well stay here. I'm sure we're not the only ones who want lunch." Alice placed her paddle on the seat and walked over to Peggy, standing in the back.

Annie watched the women chat for a bit before giving the room another scan. She noted that Stella was no longer in her seat, but Mary Beth still occupied hers. Gwendolyn continued her service in the snack area. And Kate was nowhere to be seen.

When Alice returned, she had good news. "Peggy is about to go on duty. If we wait fifteen or twenty minutes, she'll do her best to fit us in. So that gives us a chance to pay for our purchases; then we'll go for lunch."

They stood in a short line to run credit cards and then left. Soon they waited at the entrance of the Cup and Saucer with a few other folks. Motioning for Annie to stay in line, Alice stepped inside. When she peeked out, she beckoned Annie forward.

"We have to share a table," Alice said, as Peggy led them across the packed restaurant. "But I think this is going to work. It's with Kate and Vanessa."

"What? How did you manage that?" Annie was both pleased and frightened. How would Kate react? Did she know they were joining her?

"Peggy felt you two needed to talk. So she's behind this little conspiracy." Alice squeezed Annie's hand. As they approached the table, Vanessa looked up in shock.

"Vanessa, why don't you slip over there next to your mother, so we can double up with another couple of customers?" Peggy said with cheer she probably didn't feel.

Trying not to make more eye contact, the teen slid out of the booth and moved in next to Kate.

Peggy laid a couple of menus on the table. "Ladies? Enjoy your meal."

"Hi, Kate. Thanks for making room," Alice said, sliding into the vacant bench. "I'm starving."

Annie took a deep breath and slid in next to Alice. "Me, too."

Kate stared at Annie. "We're leaving."

— 17 —

"But Mom! We can't leave now!" Vanessa held her seat as Kate tried to slide out of the booth. "We already ordered." Her look appeared one of desperation. And resolve.

"Vanessa, move over," Kate said, flashing an intense sideways look that seemed to signal a warning. She pushed again, but her daughter didn't budge. "Vanessa!"

"No, no, I'll leave," Annie said, getting up.

"You're not going anywhere." Alice pulled her down. "And neither are you, Kate. It's time you two talked. Past time." She looked from Kate to Annie and back again.

Kate glared across the table as Alice continued. "Now, you're both going to sit here and talk. Peggy arranged this meeting because she cares for both of you and doesn't like what's happening. This is destroying our Hook and Needle group. Annie's about at the end of her tether, and I've definitely had enough! Vanessa, what about you?"

Watching Alice, the teen stared wide-eyed. She nodded her agreement in silence.

"There, you see? Even our Stony Point children are in agreement. Vanessa, come with me." Alice stood and waited for Vanessa to wrench herself out of the booth. "You women have something to talk about. Vanessa and I will just sit at those two open spots at the counter.

Then you can have your privacy. Bon appétit."

Alice had made it happen. Here was Annie's opportunity.

"Can we talk, Kate? Just for a few minutes?"

Kate didn't reply, instead staring out the window.

I'll take that as a green light. Annie struggled to remember just how to start.

"I've noticed that we've become a bit distant all of a sudden."

Well, that was an understatement. She needed to focus or Kate would end the conversation before it began.

Annie tried again. "I've been bothered by the gap growing between us." For some reason, her speech seemed silly and rehearsed.

Kate now stared at Annie. "Don't think being Betsy's granddaughter will get you off. I'm still not talking to you." She crossed her arms and looked away.

"But why? Can't you tell me why? Please let me make it right, Kate!" Annie swallowed hard. "I. . .I miss you."

Kate's dropped her eyes. "I simply couldn't believe it. But it's unforgivable. I can't overlook it."

"What in the world are you talking about?" Annie stared at Kate, perplexed.

Kate shook her head. "When Harry told me that you'd been flirting with him, hitting on him actually, well—" Kate gave Annie an agonized look. "Don't you know I'm still not over him? How could you? I thought you were my friend!"

"Me? Flirting with Harry? You mean. . .your ex-husband?" Annie struggled to understand. And why would anyone say such a thing about her? And why would Harry, whom she had never met? It defied all logic.

"Oh, Kate! It isn't true. I've never even met him, never spoken to him, never seen him, never before that night at the Fish House." Annie's eyes burned and she blinked back tears.

"What are you saying?" Kate sat up straight. "That Harry is lying?"

Annie couldn't agree out loud. She reworded her response.

"I'm saying it's only been a year since Wayne passed away. He was the love of my life. My heart is broken, Kate. I'm not interested in anyone else! Certainly not now, and maybe not ever." Her voice wavered and a single tear spilled down her cheek. "I miss my husband every minute of every day."

Kate was quiet and then finally spoke. "Of course. I didn't think about that when Harry said all those things about you and him. Well, when he lied to me." Kate looked defeated. "I guess I fell for his line again. . .believed him again."

"I can tell you still care for him, too," Annie said, her kindness genuine. Sometimes it can take a long time for love to fade.

"God help me, I do. The scoundrel. What I don't understand is why he would accuse you of coming on to him."

"Maybe it was a mistake. Maybe he thought I was someone else."

"I doubt it," Kate said. Then her gaze softened. "Annie,

I'm so sorry! I've done a terrible thing, setting our friends against you. I guess my pride kept me from confronting you with the whole story. Which turned out to be another of Harry's lies. Can you forgive me?"

Relief washed over Annie. "Of course I forgive you. And it's all forgotten, too. Friends don't hold grudges," she said, patting Kate's hand. "Now let's order lunch. I'm starved."

Alice and Vanessa returned to the table, and soon they all plunged into the cook's special, fish and chips. By the time Peggy delivered a huge hot fudge sundae with four spoons on the side, the mood in that particular booth radiated amity. Annie couldn't remember when she'd last felt so light of heart.

"Did you find anything at the auction, Kate?" Annie asked, thinking about the other items that still tempted her, the box of frames in particular. Maybe she and Alice could dash back before the frames were history.

Kate glanced at her daughter. "I bid on a cute side table for Vanessa's room. The style seemed Victorian to me, though I don't know my antiques like you, Alice."

"Was it two-tiered and kind of. . .well, battered?" Alice probed for details as she spooned up some fudge-covered ice cream. "If so, you are spot on."

"That's the one. But I plan to freshen it up with some paint. Which reminds me, we better go get it and get going," Kate said, glancing at her daughter. "It's Harry's turn to have Vanessa for the weekend. I have a few things I want to discuss with him."

"Oh-oh." Annie didn't even want to know about

this conversation. "Remember, he might have made a mistake."

"He'd better hope he did. Believe me." Kate's tone told everyone she was more than serious. She slid out of the booth after her daughter and tucked some bills under the salt shaker. "But first, I have to talk with some Hook and Needle friends."

Annie grinned. Then she remembered something. "Speaking of the Hook and Needlers, can I ask you something before you go?"

"Anything."

"Well, earlier this week, they had figured out that I found something from World War II in Gram's attic."

"I remember." Kate raised her brows. "So we were right?"

"On target. I found military medals with no owner," Annie answered. "Do you know if Harry's grandfather was a war hero?"

"Pops? No way. He did serve during the war, but he never talks about it. Harold Stevens is the meekest man I've ever known." Kate covered Vanessa's ears in jest. "He's no hero. . .war or otherwise."

"Mom!" Vanessa pulled her mother's hands away. "I'm not a baby."

"Of course not. But you're my baby," Kate said, dismissing the complaint. "So Annie, does this mean I can discuss the World War II medals with the others?"

"Discuss away," Annie said. "I'm especially interested to know if there was a local boy who became a hero. Perhaps you could talk to Harry—"

"Oh, I'll be talking to Harry all right. Don't worry about that." Kate's eyes narrowed.

"Do you mind if I talk to Harold? He is your family, after all. I did a little sleuthing and found out he lives at Ocean View Assisted Living," Annie said.

"Why didn't you just ask me? I could have told you that!" Kate said; then she grew thoughtful. "Oh. I guess you couldn't talk to me, could you?"

"That's behind us, remember?" Annie smiled. "Alice and I were talking about Harold last night at dinner and decided we should explore all of the information he is willing to share. What if he has an important clue?"

Alice spoke up then. "And maybe Stella knows something, too. I bet she might be able to clarify some of what happened back then."

"Absolutely. Talk to Stella. And talk to Harold with my blessing. He's a sweet old guy. Oh, this is so exciting. Consider me on the case," Kate said, her good humor returning as she winked at Annie and then sobered. "And thanks. . .for being so forgiving."

Annie waved her off and, as Kate and Vanessa left to pay their bill, turned to Alice. "Thank you for making this happen. I'm so glad it's over."

"Me, too. Now we can go back to normal."

"That sounds like heaven." Annie dug in her purse for some cash. "Alice, this is my treat. I owe you so much more than a free lunch."

"Nonsense! But thanks. Let's hurry back to the church and see what's left. Maybe that Autoharp is still up for grabs."

The crowd had thinned by half when they returned to the auction. Tommy O'Connor's voice still rang out over the speakers, calling a bidding war between two Autoharp devotees. "Fifteen dollars. Fifteen dollars. This is a good deal folks. Who will give me twenty?"

"Twenty!" Alice called out and then clapped her hand over her mouth. Annie laughed and wandered over to the boxed lots that were left, pleased to see that the frames had not yet gone up for bid.

Where was Gram's pillow? It must have already sold. Disappointed to miss that sale, Annie looked for her afghans among the boxes and couldn't find them either.

She did a scan of the room and realized that none of the other friends remained. Even Gwendolyn was gone, having done more than her share of volunteer work, in Annie's opinion. She wondered if they were all with Kate and smiled at the idea.

After Alice had won her Autoharp and Annie the frames, they paid for their items and walked outside to where volunteers were stacking auction items for pickup. Wally worked among the helpers, waving at them between boxes.

"Let's take the small stuff with us and then bring the car around for your chair. I'll have to see if someone can deliver my dresser," Alice said.

To her surprise, Annie saw her chair being carried out by Ian Butler. "Isn't this a bit beyond your job description, Mr. Mayor?"

"I think everyone helping out is going beyond his or her comfort zone. But that's Stony Point. Volunteerism is second nature to these folks." He sat the chair down and grinned. "Nice buy, Annie. Too bad about the broken leg. But I bet Wally can fix it for you."

So that was the reason Annie had gotten the chair so cheap. The broken leg. This was the chair Annie had meant to skip. Quickly checking her item list, she saw no note at all next to that lot number. She recalled when the chair had come up for bid. It looked perfect from the fifth row. Annie had been so excited that Miss Blue Top hadn't bid on this one that she bid without checking her list. Not that it would have helped.

"Wally does seem able to fix anything," Annie said, hoping she was right. Walking around the chair, she examined the defect. What could she do but make the best of it? "Once the leg is repaired, it will look great on my porch. Whenever I sit in it, I'll remember my first auction experience in Stony Point."

Mike Malone brought out the box of frames and the Autoharp. Alice took it from him and held it like a baby. "I am so pleased that I bid on this. Just wait until I'm an Autoharp virtuoso." She strummed a C chord with her fingernails. It was out of tune.

"I think that can be fixed," Annie said, wincing a little. "But I'm not sure Wally can help in this case."

Ian relieved Mike of the box of frames and set them in the chair. "Annie, I was about to call it a day. May I walk you to your car? Perhaps I could get a glimpse of those medals before you go."

Ian's input could bring her one step closer to solving the mystery.

"Sure. Then I'll bring the car back and pick up the chair. It might fit into the back seat." Annie said. "Once I take those bulky medals out."

"If the chair doesn't fit, Ms. Dawson, I can bring it by for you. I'll be doing deliveries tomorrow afternoon. That includes your dresser, Alice. Look for it around three o'clock," Mike said before he disappeared into the building.

Alice, hugging her Autoharp, walked beside Annie and the mayor to the edge of the church parking lot, parting company so Alice could cross over to the lot at the town hall. The women said a quick farewell, and Annie and Ian continued the short distance to her car.

As they approached it, Ian rubbed his hands together in anticipation. "This is all so intriguing. I wonder if we'll be able to declare some unknown serviceman a hero. Wouldn't that be something?"

"I have those photos, too. The man in uniform and the young woman. You might recognize someone from your knowledge of Stony Point history." Annie placed her hand on the back-door handle. "Don't let me forget, I may have some new information."

Ian nodded. "If you are free, we can walk over to the Cup and Saucer for coffee and a chat. Though it's been busy over there all day."

"Like a beehive with Queen Peggy running the show." Annie pulled open the car door and leaned in to retrieve the medals from the back seat.

They were gone.

~ 18 ~

Annie thought she must be seeing things. Or *not* seeing things. Where were the medals? They *had* to be there. Frantic, she felt around with her hand, running fingers between the backrest and seat. Not that the case was slim enough to disappear into the depths of the bench seat. Nothing on the floor, either. Annie stuck her hand under the front seat and patted around, hoping.

Could she have taken a wild turn or stopped suddenly and the medals slid across the upholstery, falling between the other door and the seat? Not likely.

"Can I help?" Ian asked, his voice intruding upon her search. And her anxiety.

She backed out of the car doorway, completely baffled. "They're missing. The medals, the photos, even the file with Grandpa Holden's military records. Gone."

"Are you sure?" Ian shifted the box of frames. "Could they be at Grey Gables?"

"Of course I'm sure!" Annie's voice betrayed the irritation she felt. "I never took them into the house. Obviously, I should have."

Ian looked concerned. "Annie, this just doesn't happen in Stony Point. Folks don't usually lock their doors, even at their homes. We pride ourselves on our honesty."

"That's what I've always heard." But she also knew thefts happen every day.

Just not in Stony Point, Maine.

The mayor thought a moment. "Could you have moved them to the trunk?"

She shook her head, adamant. "No. I would have remembered. Besides, I loaded my auction donations into the trunk yesterday and the medals weren't there." Annie tried to quell the growing anger inside. Why would anyone want such personal items? And how could she have been so careless? Gram and Grandpa protected those medals for many years. With good reason, she was sure.

Annie had found and lost them in under a week.

"How about I put these frames in your trunk, since it's empty?" He transferred the weight of the box back to the other arm.

"Oh, sorry." Annie walked to the rear of the car and popped the latch with her remote key. She opened it and looked into every corner, just to be sure they weren't there. "It's not entirely empty, but there's plenty of room. Thanks for carrying them all this way."

"No problem." Ian dropped the heavy box into the space. "There, that should ride home just fine."

She wasn't sure what to do next. Should she report the theft to the police? The need to involve them in her previously safe little world made her uneasy. Why would anyone take these particular items—the medals and photos and file?

Were they of any value?

She couldn't answer that question. Not yet.

"Annie?" Ian had closed the trunk and now stood watching her. "What can I do to help? I'll be glad to go with you to the police station and fill out a report. Or would you like to get your bearings? Talk about it a little first?"

"I'd rather talk it out, figure it out, if I can. Maybe I'll take you up on that cup of coffee. But first, let me take another look." Annie circled the car, opening all the doors and checking under all the seats for the stolen items.

She frowned, biting her lip. Then she shrugged her shoulders and turned back to Ian. "Just needed to satisfy myself that I was thorough."

They started toward the Cup and Saucer, and then Annie stopped. She spun around, pointed her remote key toward the Malibu, and clicked the doors locked before rejoining the mayor in their trek.

The two walked in silence, Annie running questions through her mind, and Ian apparently respecting her need to do so. The temperature had cooled and a brisk wind carried a briny scent on its breath. By the time they reached the restaurant, they both were craving a cup of something steamy.

They found a table amid the bustling diners. The efficient Peggy had menus in front of them before they even saw her coming. Ian asked for a cup of coffee and as many refills as he was allowed. Annie ordered a tall hot chocolate with a mound of whipped cream on top.

"Comfort food," she said, a hint of a grin interrupting her gloom.

"I'll top that," Ian said and ordered a basket of French fries before Peggy left. "Even more comfort food. To share."

How could anyone remain glum in Ian's company? Besides, the day had been mostly delightful up until twenty minutes ago. The auction experience was one she'd never forget. Her new wicker chair had been won at a bargain price, a deal in spite of the broken leg. And reuniting with Kate had gladdened her heart. Annie smiled.

"That's better," he said. "Now, Mrs. Dawson, why don't you tell me what you've learned since I saw you last?"

"I've learned there are thieves in Stony Point." So much for her mood switch. Though Annie wanted to focus on the best parts of the day, thoughts of the theft tainted her view.

"As your mayor, I am troubled by that." Ian pushed his cup over to catch the stream of coffee Peggy poured. "This is not a reputation I ever wanted attached to our town. That's not who we are . . ."

Annie sighed, pulling her cup of chocolate near. "Maybe it's just a visiting auction enthusiast. Someone from out of town who took the opportunity to pinch some interesting bits of history."

"We'll see, Annie. If I hear a lot of reports of petty thefts from the afternoon's event, yes, it will indicate someone working the parking lots."

"Not a Stony Point resident then."

"Right." Ian sipped his coffee, frowning a little. "However, if yours is the only theft, it was on purpose. Someone wanted to take them."

"But no one knew about the medals except Alice," Annie said. Of course the Hook and Needle Club knew about a World War II item, thanks to Alice's slip of the tongue at the yarn shop. But they didn't know about the medals. Maybe another local person did.

Wait. Annie had forgotten about Grace Emory, the Stony Point librarian. Grace knew. And the mayor knew. Annie had told him at the park. She gave him a guarded glance. Then shook off that notion. If ever there was a straight arrow, it had to be Ian Butler.

Maybe she had mentioned it to someone else.

What if it was the real owner of the medals? Suppose he came to claim them at last? But why not just come to Annie and explain his story?

Ian observed her as she considered these questions. "When we met on Wednesday, you'll recall I had already heard about your World War II mystery in the attic. Perhaps by today the thief had heard about it, as well."

"That makes sense." Annie stirred her chocolate, thoughtfully. "When I saw that the medals were gone, it occurred to me that the mystery was finished. There were no medals to return to their rightful owner."

"Is that your decision, then? To end your search?" Ian waited for her answer.

After a short silence, she said, "If anything, I'm more determined to find out the whole story. It's more than curiosity. I'm involved now."

"Good for you!" He raised his cup in a mock salute. "I'm glad you want to continue the search. Besides, it bothers me to think that one of our residents may have lost something so meaningful. I'd like to see them restored to their rightful owner."

"I so wish Gram was here to ask . . ." Annie said, still stirring her chocolate.

"I'm sure there are many questions you have for her," Ian said. "Certainly Betsy Holden could clear up this mystery right now." He moved his coffee to the side. "Good news. Our French fries are here."

Peggy placed the basket on their table. "Careful. Hot out of the deep fryer." She pushed a squeeze bottle of ketchup toward the middle and topped off Ian's coffee with the other hand. "Anything else I can get you?"

Annie reached for the waitress's hand, delaying her dash to another table. "Peggy, thanks for arranging the conversation with Kate this afternoon. Things are back to normal, thanks to you and Alice."

"That is good news," Peggy said, her expression even more cheerful than before. "So that means we're back on the case? The whole Hook and Needle Club?" She took a pad and pen out from the pocket of her pink uniform. "I'd better start jotting down suspicious chatter. You never know what you might learn at the Cup and Saucer."

"I bet," Annie said. "You'll get the straight scoop at the next meeting."

Peggy hurried away to help other customers, and Annie helped herself to a crispy fry. Dipping it into a spot of ketchup and crunching absently, she decided Ian was right. Here was real comfort food. And to her surprise, she did feel comforted. Perhaps it was the food, or the friendship, or both. Her distress began to slip away, making room for the mystery to take its place in her thoughts once more.

"So what *have* you found out?" Ian asked again. "Let's have it all. I have plenty of refills left."

Annie considered the question. "All I've uncovered is that Harold Stevens lives at Ocean View Assisted Living. I plan to visit him and find out if he knew Gram or Grandpa. He must have. They were all about the same age. Maybe he'll have some new information for us."

"Good idea. If Harold was in the war, he might have known your grandfather back then. Though it's doubtful that they were on the same ship at the same time."

"Why not? Couldn't that happen?" Annie asked.

Ian nodded. "Of course. But I think it's unlikely. Remember, your grandfather was on the hospital ship, the USS *Beneficent*. I've known Harold for some time and never heard that he had any medical skills."

"So Harold must have been on another ship."

"That's my guess. Or stationed on a base somewhere. Though I've never heard him talk about it." Ian squinted, as if looking for an elusive fact. "Can't say I've ever seen him on a VFW float on Veteran's Day, either."

"He must be a very private person." Annie took a last fry. "Right now, if it's still open, I'd like to stop by the library and see if Grace has anything for me about Grandpa Holden. She did an interlibrary loan request to High Falls, Connecticut, his home town. Maybe whatever they send will give us a clue."

Checking his watch, Ian said, "You better get over there. They close early on Saturdays. I'll walk you part of the way. Then I want to stop by the police station."

"Oh, please don't say anything about the theft yet. Maybe the medals will turn up. Probably just some kids playing army or something."

"Do you really believe that?"

"No. But I'm not ready to go to the authorities. I'll just lock my car," Annie said and stood. "And my house."

"I hate to say it," he said, standing as well, "but maybe you should."

Annie knew that Ian's caution came as a result of his concern, but it affected her like a scene from a scary movie. She shuddered. It would take more than chocolate and French fries to make her feel comfortable again in Stony Point.

~ 19 ~

After waving good-bye to the mayor at the corner of Main Street and Oak Lane, Annie power-walked the short distance to the Stony Point Library. Without stopping to admire the noble structure, she pushed past the paned door and hurried into the empty Great Room, heading straight to the circulation desk.

Behind the counter, a fifty-something blond woman looked up from her task, her smile a welcome. Pinned on the lapel of her blue jacket was a gold badge, its engraved black letters reading "Valerie Duffy, Circulation Librarian."

"I'm sorry to tell you we are about to close." Valerie looked sympathetic as she pushed up her oversized glasses. She glanced up at the wall clock, meaningfully.

Because time was running out, Annie didn't waste any. "Is Grace Emory around?" she asked, her gaze sweeping the room.

"Sorry, Grace already left for the day. Is there anything I can do to help?"

"Maybe. She did an interlibrary loan request for me on Wednesday, and I'm wondering if she's received anything back yet."

"By any chance, are you Annie Dawson?"

When Annie said she was, the librarian pulled a

wooden tray labeled "ILL Returns" from a shelf behind the counter. She lifted a manila envelope from the top of a small stack and handed it over.

"Here it is," she said. "Right on top. I just left you a message on your answering machine, which you can disregard now, of course."

"That was fast. I'm impressed," Annie said, examining the envelope. "And pleased."

"Grace e-mailed your request to Connecticut to speed up the process." Valerie said. "And they faxed back all this information to us. A quick turnaround."

"Please relay my thanks to Mrs. Emory." Annie's hands shook with excitement. "I know you're closing soon. Do I have enough time to glance over these before I go? I don't think I can wait until I get home."

"No problem. We have fifteen minutes left. Which reminds me! I have to make the closing announcement. Though there isn't anyone here but us. And Ted, the security guard. There are empty tables right over there where you can spread your things out."

The librarian disappeared through a door behind her desk, and Annie quickly found a seat near the entrance. She tossed her purse on a nearby chair. Turning over the envelope, she ripped open the flap, mangling it in her rush to see inside.

Annie drew out a number of papers that appeared to be photocopies of Charlie Holden's history as a boy and young man in Connecticut. The pages consisted of local articles describing Grandpa's prowess on the football field, his role in the high school play, graduation photos, enlistment notification, and finally, his wedding announcement.

All interesting stuff, but not much about the war and not a hint about the medals. No surprise, really. So far, the evidence had pointed to Harold instead of Grandpa. Sighing, Annie put the papers back into the envelope and tried to reseal the flap. She gathered her belongings and began to amble out the door. No need to hurry now. Then she stopped.

Beelining back to the circulation desk, Annie's impatience returned and she tapped her fingers on the Formica countertop, waiting for Ms. Duffy to reappear from behind the door. Over the public address system, Valerie's clear tones delivered news to no one.

"May I have your attention, please? The library will close in fifteen minutes. Save your work on the computers now; they shut down automatically. If you have materials to check out, please do so immediately. Thank you."

When Valerie emerged, at last, Annie's fingernail tapping came to an abrupt halt.

"Grace received great information, but not exactly what I needed." An understatement, to be sure. "Could I get some help with another search?" With the last-minute drop-by, the nail tapping, and now another request, Annie felt she might be inching over the library etiquette line. Just a bit.

"Sure," Valerie said, still cheerful in spite of the hour's lateness. "But we won't be able to initiate it until Monday morning. Can you stop by then? If we need to do another ILL, we will. But maybe you can find what you need right here." She waved her arm toward the reference room. "We only have ten minutes. I really can't stay longer or our security guard goes on overtime."

Annie realized she'd stepped well over that imaginary etiquette line now. Her search would simply have to wait until Monday. She and Alice had planned to talk to the Veterans of Foreign Wars group then, anyway. However, because the medals had vanished, perhaps they would reconsider the visit.

Before Annie could offer thanks, Valerie slipped through the office door again. Probably more end-of-the-day announcements to proclaim.

Annie turned toward the exit where Security Guard Ted busied himself locking the door. He held it open for her. "Good-night, Miss."

It had been some time since Annie been called "miss," but she enjoyed wearing the label one more time. The term contained a genteel spirit she found rather sweet. Just the sort of thing she'd always experienced in Stony Point.

Her walk back to her car was brisk. Purposeful. Wasn't that the right way to thwart a thief? Recalling an old habit, Annie pulled out her keys and positioned them between her fingers—a weapon to the unsuspecting stalker. Almost like having a set of brass knuckles, only in her case, it was spiky knuckles. Without the Mafia ties.

As she strolled, every step one of fake bravado, she thought how out of place she felt, trying to arm herself against an unknown threat in this dear little coastal town. Someone had broken into her car and taken the medals. But was that all he wanted?

Once safely locked inside Grey Gables with her box of frames and Boots purring on her lap, she called Alice. She must have had plans for the evening; Annie had to leave a message. After giving a brief rundown on the theft, she asked Alice to call as soon as she arrived home, no matter how late. Annie wanted to plot their next strategy. Not so easy without the medals.

Next she called LeeAnn in Texas, needing to hear her familiar voice. Annie, anxious to update her about a first auction experience, began to describe the event.

"You wouldn't believe it, LeeAnn. There was a woman who bid on all this wonderful wicker furniture and wouldn't allow anyone else to win even one piece! Wasn't that rude?"

"*So* rude. What a wicker-hog." LeeAnn said, apparently empathizing. "Did you get to bid on anything?"

"I got a whole box of old frames. They all have that thick glass, too. I plan to paint a couple to frame the pictures the twins did."

"Neat," LeeAnn said. "Anything else?"

"Well—" Annie couldn't lie, though the impulse danced across her mind. "I bought one more thing, but it turned out to be broken."

"Broken? Didn't you preview, Mom? What was it?"

Annie flinched as she held the phone. "It was a. . .wicker chair."

There was a long silence on the line. Finally, LeeAnn said, "I see. So that rude woman didn't buy every piece of wicker. Just every good piece."

"You put that so succinctly." Annie smiled now at her

inept auction ability. "As they say, live and learn. Besides, I'm pretty sure Wally can fix it. In the end, I think I'll have a gorgeous wicker chair for very little money."

"Way to go, Mom. You always could take care of yourself. What a woman."

Annie laughed. "Not sure if I can take much credit. Alice came to my aid over and over. But things do have a way of working out, don't they?"

They continued their conversation, Annie even chatting with both John and Joanna for a few minutes before LeeAnn got back on the phone. The visit was a better balm to what ailed her than the biggest basket of French fries. Annie informed LeeAnn on the kitchen remodel, detailing Wally's work so far. She didn't, however, fill her in on the thievery thing. No need to upset the poor dear.

Or start an argument.

They ended their conversation with Annie promising to look at dates for returning to Texas. The holidays would be here before she had a chance to buy her plane ticket, according to LeeAnn. Or. . .her mom could just pack up before the weather turned wintry and drive home. For good.

That LeeAnn is a persuasive young woman.

When Annie hung up the phone, she pressed the button on the answering machine. As promised, librarian Valerie Duffy had left a message that the interlibrary loan item had arrived.

Mike Malone spoke next. "Ms. Dawson, just a confirmation that I'm doing deliveries tomorrow afternoon, weather permitting. Should be by your place between three and four o'clock. If you're not home, I'll leave your chair on the porch."

Another message elicited funds for a particular candidate running for the Stony Point school board in the fall. Goodness, who was she? And why had she called Annie?

Lifting her sleeping cat to her chest, Annie gave her a snuggle and then arranged her on the sofa. Boots barely awakened, only opening one eye halfway before relaxing into the cushion like a floppy feline doll.

Annie headed upstairs to change, pulling off her sweater and accidentally hooking the pearl necklace around her chin. Once it fell back into place, she ran the pendant back and forth along the gold chain as she selected a sage-colored T-shirt to wear for the evening. Just as well that the expensive trinket hadn't been exposed all afternoon if a thief had targeted her.

Or had her car been one of many? She wondered what Ian had learned at the police station. It might be too soon for folks to notice things missing from their vehicles. If Annie hadn't opened her back door with the intention of showing the medals to the mayor, who knows how long before she would have realized they were gone?

In fact, how long *had* they been gone? When had she seen them last? Thursday was her best guess. She'd taken them to Ian's office. Then placed them on her back seat and spent time in town.

She'd been to town several times since then. Parked her car at Alice's, at the church, at the assisted-living facility, at Magruder's, and places she couldn't recall.

What if the medals and other items hadn't been taken

during the auction at all? She could be wrong about what happened today, overreacting to an imaginary crime.

Or she could be a target.

A loud knock on the front door startled Annie. She quickly stepped into her jeans. Unclasping her necklace, she dropped it into an antique bowl filled with earrings she hadn't yet put away. She shrugged on the long-sleeved T-shirt and dashed back to the landing.

"Coming! Coming!" Annie said in response to more knocking, taking the steps as fast as she could.

She opened the door wide, breathless.

"Don't you ever look first to see who it is before flinging open your door?" Alice stood with hands on hips, her stare reproving. She wagged her finger. "After having your things stolen right out of your car—what if I were the perp?"

Annie tried not to laugh. "The perp?"

"You know what I mean," Alice said, striding through the hallway and into the living room. She dropped her cross-stitch bag on the floor with a thump. Boots, apparently interrupted from her sweet sleep, refused to acknowledge the visitor and jumped off the sofa. The cat trotted out into the hall, tail held high, and disappeared.

Alice plumped up a pillow and settled into the corner Boots had vacated. "Annie, have a seat."

"I thought that was my line," Annie said, sitting in a floral chair across from her friend.

"Okay, you got me there. But is it my fault that you are such a good hostess, hospitality just exudes from the whole house? You don't even need to try; I already feel welcomed when I turn into the driveway." Alice opened her bag and pulled out her current cross-stitch project.

"Oh, please." Annie laughed, though she indeed was pleased that Alice felt that way. "I knew you were at the door. Who else would it be?"

"That's the question. Who? Or is that whom?" Alice rolled her eyes upward, as if looking for the answer on the ceiling. "No matter. Annie, I'm worried about you. I'm afraid you might be in real danger."

"I don't think having those medals stolen out of my car warrants a bodyguard. Though I do wonder why just those items were stolen."

"It is weird to think that someone we don't know examined your grandfather's file and looked at the photos, too," Alice said, stitching on her design.

Annie nodded. "I get nervous thinking about it. Plus I feel terrible to have lost those medals and pictures after my grandparents kept them safe for so long."

Alice stopped her stitching. "You're not the person at fault here, Annie. Someone else helped himself, or herself, to those medals. That's the person to blame."

"Do you think it could be a woman?" Annie wondered if anyone in her circle of friends might have a reason to make off with the medals.

But, no. She wouldn't even entertain such a scenario. The idea was absurd.

"Hmm." Alice considered it. "I know they've been a little persnickety lately, but I can't imagine anybody in our Hook and Needle Club ever hurting you or taking your property. They aren't that sort. Besides they were all devoted to Betsy. She gives you an additional shield of protection."

Gram again. Her loveliness lived on, reaching out and covering Annie with its sweetness. It made her feel both grateful for her heritage and embarrassed that she had lost the medals. Like she broke a trust.

They chatted as they stitched until it was time for Alice to leave. Annie watched her get into the Mustang, fire it up with a respectable roar, and drive away. She didn't want anything happening to her best friend.

That night Annie turned from side to side, never finding just the right position for a sound sleep. Her thoughts would not rest either. It was a scary experience for her to be the victim of a theft. Or any kind of victim. She didn't like the word. It made her feel powerless when she had just begun to gain control again.

What if Annie had learned something no one ever wanted divulged? Something kept secret with the medals for all these years? What if she truly was a target?

Annie pulled the covers up around her ears. If only Wayne were here. No one would dare harm her then.

Shivering, she dragged Boots across the quilt and hugged her close.

~ 20 ~

Annie spent most of Sunday hunkered down at the house, avoiding all thoughts of medals. She needed a little time off, even from church, and started the day locked safely indoors.

Mike Malone had called to cancel his chair delivery, suffering from a sore back after loading boxes for one-too-many auction customers. Alice had been busy all day, so Annie's interactions were at a minimum, the phone ringing only one other time, a call from her grand-children. At home in her cozy world, she painted two of the vintage frames with some gloss white paint Wally had left behind. Then with Boots as company, she settled down to finish her afghan. A minor masterpiece, if Annie did say so. Too bad it was a day late for the auction. Now she'd have to find it a new home. Most likely, the afghan was Texas bound.

Should she be bound for home, as well?

Restless, Annie looked around for another project but found nothing to tempt her. Rather than pace up and down the hallway, she decided to take a drive along the harbor. Perhaps she would pull over and walk among the boats, allowing the lapping waves to lull her troubled spirit. But before she realized it, Annie had passed the pier and pointed her Malibu toward Ocean View Assisted Living. And Harold Stevens.

The senior facility sprawled across a hillside just outside of town, overlooking the ocean. She parked in the guest lot and sauntered along the sidewalk, trying to glimpse the sea view beyond lush lawns. But the view was blocked by a low wall at the edge of the cliff. Nearby stone benches sat angled toward the water, a rustic vista point.

She made a decision. Instead of entering the Ocean View Assisted Living campus through the security gate, Annie turned and followed the signs toward the benches. She mused that it might not be so bad to live in a senior home if one had such a view.

The bench was hard and cold, and she sat scrutinizing the wild waves churning like fluid fury. She'd like to get a closer look, but gathering gray clouds hung like a menace, threatening to storm. From the scent of the sea air, she sensed there was little time before rain would fall. So she hurried toward the rock wall, wanting to better take in the magnificent sight but dreading the thought of being trapped in a downpour.

What was that? She swirled around, certain she had heard something. Or someone. But the grounds were empty. Annie stood alone, with only a cluster of old oaks bending at odd angles to keep her company. Why was she so jumpy?

She shook it off. She saw no other people, not even a dog prowling about. At this moment only Annie was enjoying this particular sight. Annie. . .and a number of seniors who might also be looking out from the facility's wall of windows facing the Atlantic.

To the right of the wall stood a sign pointing to a cliff-walk down to a lower landing where seals might be seen at play. Intrigued, Annie walked along the rocky barrier, stones stacked one on top of another. It didn't look all that secure. Following the sign's direction, she stepped onto a narrow stone path. Edging her way downward, she held on to a metal railing attached to the side of the sea cliff. On her right, the ocean view was unobstructed. It was both exhilarating and frightening. She hadn't done anything like this in Texas.

Annie stopped midway down the walk to watch the stirring sea splash against the rocks. A light mist covered her clothes as she basked in the primal feeling of the ocean. Her sights focused on Butler's Lighthouse. The proverbial light in the storm. She wished she had her camera.

A loud rumble from overhead interrupted her reverie. She jerked her head back in time to see something tumbling toward her. Landslide! Annie's hand slipped off the slick railing as she dodged the oncoming rocks. Teetering on the edge of the slippery stones, Annie almost lost her balance. She managed to again grab the railing, evading a plunge onto the rocky terrain below.

Breathless, she waited until the landslide subsided. She leaned back against the cliff, heart pumping like rapid cannon fire, and clung to the railing with both hands. A few minutes passed before Annie was able to inch her way back up the path. At the top, she collapsed on one of the stone benches. But she no longer cared about the view.

What had started the landslide? Or who? Looking around, she still saw no one. Her attention turned to the rock wall. Could some rocks have simply loosened and knocked others free as they fell? From the bench, she couldn't see anything amiss. She probably wouldn't anyway, because she lacked the nerve to explore so close to the drop. In this case, ignorance was her security.

The skies darkened even more. The rain should start soon, as if to punctuate Annie's disastrous adventure. Dampness from the mist had crept into her clothes and chilled her bones. Shaken, it seemed past time to head over to Ocean View Assisted Living and seek out Harold Stevens. She hurried through the security gate, which she deemed a wise idea, considering the cliff-walk. Easy to enter but maybe not so easy to leave.

Annie noticed a lovely wreath on the door with a sign beneath that read "Welcome home to Ocean View." She entered and found the receptionist. After asking about Harold Stevens, she was led through a hall into a large room, its amazing oceanic vista even better than Annie expected. A group of seniors played bingo at a long table, the numbers called out by a woman who must have been the activities director.

To the side, a resident sat alone, gazing through the wall of windows out to sea.

"Harold, you have a visitor," the receptionist said, touching his shoulder before leaving to assist a frail woman whose walker wouldn't go forward.

"Is it Harry?" the old gentleman turned and saw Annie. The light in his eyes faded. "I thought it was my grandson. He usually comes on Saturdays, but he missed yesterday."

"I'm sorry, Mr. Stevens. Maybe he'll come today, instead," Annie said, hoping she was right.

"Do you think so?" His initial regret disappeared, replaced with a hopeful smile. "Pull up a chair and meet my favorite lady, the sea." He indicated the endless ocean expanse with the sweeping wave of a gnarled hand.

Thinking of her recent close encounter with that same lady, Annie shuddered. It might be a day or two before she wanted to turn her gaze seaward again. But out of respect for the senior Mr. Stevens, she gave a courtesy glance. "It's magnificent."

"Great times, skippering my own boat. Eventually, my own fleet. Now my grandson tells the sea stories."

Annie looked at Harold, who seemed like a frail shell of what must have once been a vital seafarer. Covered by a worn afghan, he was long-limbed and still handsome. She saw the family resemblance to Kate's ex-husband Harry.

Elizabeth Taylor had just told her Harold Stevens liked the ladies. Now Annie was pretty sure the ladies must have liked him, too.

"Let me introduce myself. I'm Betsy Holden's granddaughter. Annie Dawson."

Harold's slow grin widened. "Well, I'll be. Betsy Holden. She was a sweet gal. Couldn't do no better than Betsy. We had wonderful times together."

"So you knew my grandmother well?" Annie asked.

"Oh, sure. There was a time we might have . . ." His voice trailed off, lost in memories.

"Gram used to say that she had a first love, but she never told us who."

"Is that so?" he asked, looking pleased. "Well, she was *my* first love. That's for sure. True and faithful, even though I wasn't. Best that she married Charlie."

Annie's breathing quickened. "So you knew my Grandpa Charlie, too?"

"Charlie? He was my best friend. Up until. . .well, I don't want to talk about it. It was my fault. All mine." Harold seemed to deflate before her eyes, shame washing over him.

That didn't sound right at all. Gram married her first love's best friend? *Her* Grandma Betsy? But what else could it be? The knowledge apparently embarrassed Harold. It must have ended the friendship with Charlie, though Harold seemed to take the blame. Annie again wished her grandmother were here, this time to clarify the details of her relationships with Harold and Grandpa.

Though it was really none of Annie's business.

Shifting the subject to safer ground, she said, "I just heard from someone that you were a big hit with the ladies in your youth."

Harold laughed. "I guess I was, though I don't remember most of them. I had some good years with my wife Caroline. God rest her soul. She just blotted out the rest."

"What a lovely sentiment." Annie patted his arm. Wouldn't every wife like to hear something like that?

"There was one gal, besides Betsy, that I've never forgotten. She was beautiful. With a beautiful name."

Annie must have spoken too soon. She played along, anyway. "Who was she?"

"Dorothy Divine. Doesn't that have a ring to it?"

Harold said to Annie, brightly. "Sounds like an angel."
Then he frowned. "I was in the service. So was she—a
nurse. I got myself in all kinds of trouble. Charlie tried to
help, but. . .I was in too deep."

"Tell me about that." Annie sensed that this could be
something important.

"Nope. It's private." Harold stared out the windows
again.

She sat back in her chair. What had happened all
those long years ago? Obviously Harold wasn't going to
enlighten her any further. Still. . .

"Mr. Stevens, somebody told me you were a war hero."
Okay, a white lie. But maybe somebody would. "Did you
ever receive a medal for bravery or anything?"

Harold's gaze never left his beloved sea. "Nope. I don't
have any. Didn't deserve any. That's the truth."

No wonder Kate knew nothing about his war record.
The man had just shut down at the mere mention of the
military.

"But Mr. Stevens, you served your country in wartime.
That's a fine thing, a brave thing to do, medals or not."
Annie reached out and touched his arm.

Harold stiffened. "Can't talk about it."

"Sorry. Didn't mean to pry," she said, pulling her hand
back. "But I'm very glad to have met my grandmother's
first love." Annie's voice grew gentler. "Before I go, sir, I'd
like to thank you for your service to our country."

He gave a little grunt, still staring out to sea.

When Annie left, she thought she had spotted tears in
the old gentleman's eyes.

— 21 —

Monday morning brought more blustery weather with it, an unwelcome guest for Annie to entertain when she had so much to do in town. She ventured out on the porch to gauge the temperature and then immediately hurried back into the sanctuary of Grey Gables. Cold enough for a jacket and windy enough for a gale warning. Yesterday's rain had slipped into full storm mode. Usually she found the wet weather an intriguing aspect of coastal Maine. Today it was an annoyance.

No chance Mike Malone might deliver her wicker chair today. Not in these conditions. And Wally had phoned early—taking the day off. She guessed he deserved it, after all his help at the auction. And at Grey Gables.

Annie checked her watch. Alice should be here any time now. They were headed to the community center to meet with some members of the VFW at ten o'clock sharp. Though she no longer had the medals, Annie hoped the group could help identify the unidentified one from her verbal description. Or maybe she could attempt a drawing. And these men might know about the history of Stony Point's military men and women. Who better to ask?

Anxious to be about the task, Annie pulled her navy jacket from the hall closet and tossed it across a chair. She also grabbed a long crocheted scarf of periwinkle wool to add a layer of warmth to her jeans and sweater.

Another quick glance outside to make sure Alice's Mustang wasn't idling in the driveway permitted Annie to sink onto the sofa and give Boots a few strokes.

"Lazy girl," she said, scratching behind the feline's ears. Not a care in the world. Wouldn't that be nice? "Lucky girl," she added, correcting herself.

All the events of the past couple of days rested on Annie's shoulders. The quarrel with Kate had set her on an emotional seesaw. Thank goodness they ironed out that situation. But her former distress had been replaced by the theft of the medals and the creepy avalanche yesterday at the assisted-living place. Together, they produced more than a twinge of concern for her safety. That was silly. Annie was acting as an alarmist, she knew. But she couldn't dismiss a niggling fear that something else was about to happen. Something bad.

A faint beep sounded from outside and she jumped up, waving at Alice through the window. Annie wrapped the scarf around her neck and shrugged into the coat. She picked up her purse and umbrella. After a loving good-bye pat to Boots, she dashed to the door, hand poised on the knob.

She gazed about the room one last time, appreciating all the memories made here, all she had been given. Her eyes rested on the overstuffed chair where Gram's exquisite cross-stitched pillow once lay. Had it been a mistake to donate it to the community center auction? She really missed it.

As she locked the door behind her, Annie remembered

she had no idea who had won the bid on the pillow or what price it had brought in.

No time to think about that now. She put it on her imaginary to-do list. Taking the porch steps as fast as she could without slipping, Annie rushed through the rain and into the warmth of Alice's Mustang.

During the drive into town, Annie recounted her visit with Harold. "He knew Gram. In fact, he said that she was his first love."

"Really? If that's true, Harold and Betsy could be the young couple in the picture. It was in her attic, after all. Because the photos were stored with the medal," Alice said, "he could be the owner of the Purple Heart. And that other one."

"That's what I thought, too. But when I asked him if he'd ever been awarded any World War II medals, he said no! Almost like he was angry."

"That's odd," Alice said.

"Maybe he was angry because he wasn't awarded any."

"That could explain it, I guess. He felt slighted?"

"He didn't say." Annie said. "In fact, he didn't say much of anything. He was hoping to see his grandson Harry, who usually visits Saturdays. He was just sitting there, waiting, looking out to sea."

"That's sad. He should feel great about his accomplishments: a thriving three-generation family business, a grandson to carry on the family tradition and. . .maybe some military medals."

"You're right," Annie said. "But he was so firm. Said he didn't have any medals. Didn't deserve any medals."

"Oh well, at least we've found Betsy's first love." Alice seemed placated.

Annie shifted in her seat. "I am pretty sure we have. But there's more." She told Alice how Harold had said something happened that changed things for him and Betsy. And she married his best friend, Charlie Holden.

"I don't want to think the worst. But did my grandpa somehow steal away his best friend's girl?"

"No. That can't be," Alice said. "I don't believe it."

"It's hard to imagine. But for me, this puzzle piece doesn't fit. Not when I think about the character of my grandparents." Annie looked distraught. "How could either of them be so deceitful?"

"There has to be another explanation," Alice said as she pulled into the church parking lot. She stepped out into the rain and opened her umbrella, with a wave of her hand inviting Annie to share. They darted inside.

"Look at that dear man," Alice said, as they peered around an open door. She pointed at an old gentleman in military garb typing into a computer at a long table. "I knew these people were always ready to help, through rain, sleet, or snow."

"You've got your public servants mixed up. That's the post office." Annie said. "How come he's the only one here?"

"One's all we need." Alice grabbed Annie's hand and pulled her along into the room. A small American flag hung behind the man. Next to the flag, a sign was posted: "Deeds, not words."

He looked up from beneath bushy white brows. "Good morning, ladies. I'm Commander Neil Bruce. How can an old soldier help?"

Alice nudged Annie forward.

"Well, I do have some questions, sir. . . er . . . Commander." Annie didn't know the proper protocol.

"Good. Take a seat, and I'll get out of this program," he said. "I need a break from writing this blasted post newsletter, anyway. Sure wish I knew as much about computers as my grandson. Sometimes I feel like a dunce." Shaking his head, Commander Bruce tapped the keyboard a few more times before turning toward the women, clasping his hands on the table. "You have my full attention."

Annie wasn't sure how to start. "I found this medal, two medals, actually. One is a Purple Heart. But I don't know what the other medal is." Relying on her memory, she explained how it looked.

Commander Bruce stroked his chin, thinking. "Well, why don't you just bring it by? Then I can tell you for sure."

"I don't have them anymore." A rush of embarrassment swept over her, making her face burn. Might as well cut right to the truth. "I lost them. Or more accurately, they were stolen out of my car."

"Too bad," he said. "Someone must have fallen to win that Purple Heart. He ought to have that medal to honor his sacrifice."

"She didn't lose them on purpose!" Alice raced to Annie's defense. "They were stolen, for pity's sake." She threw Annie an exasperated look.

The commander put his hands palm up. "You're right. I was just thinking out loud."

"Really, I feel terrible about the loss of the medals," Annie said. And even worse after the commander's comments. "Especially since my grandparents, Charles and Betsy Holden, kept them safe for so long."

Commander Bruce brightened. "So you're Charlie's granddaughter? Well, I'll be. Good man, Charlie. Took care of me onboard his hospital ship, the USS *Beneficent*. Because of him, I lived to polish my Purple Heart in person." He grinned mischievously. "Instead of the duty falling to my widow."

Annie sat up straight. Was this how Grandpa met Harold? Aboard a hospital ship when Harold was wounded? Of course, he hadn't said he'd been wounded, but he also said he had no medals. What if he had been hurt and taken aboard the hospital ship and placed under Grandpa's care? That would explain how the two men became friends. It made sense.

She glanced at Alice. Her excited expression told Annie they were thinking along similar lines. She turned her attention back to Commander Bruce. "I'm very proud of Grandpa Holden. And of his service."

"I'm pretty sure Charlie never got a Purple Heart. Am I correct in assuming you don't believe the medals to be his?"

Annie nodded.

"Can you draw a sketch of the other medal?" The commander found a piece of scrap paper and pushed it toward Annie, along with a pencil.

This was exactly what she had hoped to do. Annie began to draw. When she had finished her rendition of the sheriff's badge and the starred ribbon, she handed it to Alice, who took a look. "That's it," she said.

Commander Bruce pondered the picture. "That's a Medal of Honor. Awarded for extreme bravery while engaged in action against an enemy. This is serious."

"What do you mean?" Alice asked.

"Whoever stole it may be in big trouble. This particular medal is afforded special protection under federal law, and there is a big fine if anyone misuses it."

That did sound serious. Was Annie in trouble?

Was driving a Medal of Honor around in the back seat of her car and allowing it to be stolen a crime?

She swallowed hard. "I trust it will turn up. That's why we're here." Annie hoped she sounded sincere enough to keep her out of federal prison. "We definitely want to figure out the recipient's identity."

"Oh, that shouldn't be too difficult. All the Medal of Honor winners are listed on the Internet." For a non-computer-kind-of-guy, Commander Bruce seemed to know exactly what to do. "Though I couldn't take on the project myself. I can barely get out this newsletter."

"Maybe we could ask Grace Emory over at the Stony Point Library," Annie suggested. "I need to run by there, anyway."

"Good idea!" The commander nodded. "It's of the utmost importance to return the medal—both medals—to their rightful owner. And the sooner, the better. We don't want them getting into the wrong hands."

They thanked the commander and fled. Or Annie felt like they were fleeing as she rushed out of the room.

Although they had learned much, it increased her feelings of guilt. Because of her, this highly prized, government-protected medal was out there with who-knows-whom.

She hoped it wasn't too late to make amends.

"Where to next?" Alice asked, once they were tucked into the Mustang.

"Let's take that side trip to the library. We can ask Grace Emory to do a search for information about Medal of Honor winners and then . . ." Annie's voice trailed off, out of ideas.

"Good idea. We've learned a lot in the past couple of days. Or, rather, *you* have. Especially when you talked to Harold Stevens. And it's more about what he didn't say. You know?"

Annie nodded absently.

"What is it?" Alice asked, prodding her friend as she started the engine. "You have something else on your mind? I can tell."

"There is something I haven't told you," Annie said.

Alice turned off the engine. "Why not? Don't you trust me by now?"

"It isn't that. It's just that now it seems so. . .so. . .hard to believe. Like I'm being overly dramatic or something." Annie envisioned the frightening episode on that narrow stone walkway behind Ocean View Assisted Living. Boulders bouncing down unbidden, threatening to bombard her as she tried not to slip to the rocky landing below. Or was that an exaggeration of the facts? Okay, maybe it wasn't boulders, but there were some hefty rocks involved.

"It could be important."

Alice's face turned serious. "What is it?"

"Or it might be nothing."

Alice rolled her eyes. "Annie! Just tell me."

Annie related her experience—the landslide and her narrow miss with injury. Or worse. "When I looked around, I didn't see anyone. But also, I didn't see any reason for the rocks to go rushing down the hillside by themselves. I'm not sure what happened."

Alice had caught her breath as Annie described the situation at Ocean View. Now she blew it out in a relieved sigh. "I'm glad you're okay. But I think you need to be cautious, Annie. It might be nothing, as you said, but it might be a warning."

"A warning? Against what?"

"What if you are getting too close to something? What if someone is saying 'back off'?" Alice said. "What then?"

"Then I say, bring it on."

～ 22 ～

*L*et's stop at A Stitch in Time first," Annie said to Alice as they drove toward the library. "I know the usual Hook and Needle Club meeting isn't until tomorrow, but maybe we'll catch Stella. She's probably at home in this weather. But if she's in town, she'll be in the shop."

Alice didn't need a second invitation and found curbside parking only a few steps from the shop. Once inside, they hung their coats and scarves on the rack and turned to see who was in residence besides Mary Beth.

Stella sat in her comfy chair, her knitting spread across her lap. "I think the storm has done you both good." She raised one eyebrow in approval.

Mary Beth laughed and came forward to hug Annie first and then Alice. It was as if the past week had never happened.

That was fine with Annie.

"Here, girls." Mary Beth handed them some tissues to dry their faces. Soon they sat in the circle, but with no projects of their own.

"This feels unnatural," Annie said, spreading empty hands. "And I've only been here a short time. I bet you feel even odder than I do, Alice."

"Many times in my life I've felt odd." Alice's voice was expressive, as if starting a sermon. Then she stopped,

191

looking each woman in the eye before delivering her punch-
line. "But never more so than when I played a song for
Annie on my new Autoharp. I played notes that have never
been heard before. Or since. Now that, ladies, was odd."

"The woman speaks the truth," Annie said. "Though
I'm sure all we'll hear will be celestial sounds, once the
instrument is in tune."

"Thank you, my friend. I've long considered you an
Autoharp expert." Alice snuggled down into her chair,
apparently not missing her cross-stitch project at all.

Stella's knitting needles clicked along at only a mod-
erate pace, possibly because she had a question for Annie.
"A lot has happened since we last met. Kate tells us we
were right about the mystery in your attic having a direct
link to World War II. And that you found some military
medals?"

Annie sat upright, ready to cross-examine. "Yes, I did.
Sorry I wasn't ready to talk about it last week. You all
amazed me by figuring out so much with just a few clues.
Especially since I didn't mean to give out any."

Alice sank down in her chair.

Annie winked at her and said nothing.

"Regarding the medals. I wish I knew something
about them," Stella said. She looked out into the distance.
"Imagine Betsy keeping those hidden away all these years.
Or maybe it was Charlie. I wonder why?"

"Oh." Annie was disappointed. "I had hoped you might
know something."

"I'm sorry. But they are a mystery to me, as well."

"I figured you must know. Everyone told me to talk

to you: Alice, the mayor, and even Kate." Annie paused, not wanting to mention the reason she hadn't made the attempt.

Stella's face took on an empathetic look. "I understand. But that is all behind us."

Annie nodded, uncertain. "I need to tell you that the medals were stolen right out of my car. I'm not exactly sure when. It was my fault for not locking the doors."

"Nonsense! One shouldn't have to lock her doors in Stony Point. But I assure you, I will do so tonight." Indignant, Stella frowned. "You are not at fault, Annie. The thief is at fault."

"Yes. But even though they are gone, I'm more determined than ever to find their owner. Besides, Gram and Grandpa must have wanted them returned someday, or they wouldn't have guarded them for so long."

"Yes," Stella said. "Betsy was always very purposeful in everything she did."

"At first I thought it would be more difficult to put the pieces together without the medals, but I don't think I need them after all. Alice and I now know that one is the Medal of Honor. And the other one is a Purple Heart."

"Good night! A Medal of Honor? Wow," Mary Beth said.

"But that's simply not possible," Stella said, stopping her knitting and leaning forward. "How could someone from Stony Point win such a prestigious medal and no one know about it?"

Annie wondered if Stella's protest had more to do with the absence of any such historical information in the new cultural center she had opened recently. If Stella didn't feature it in her center, had it happened at all?

"We were thinking maybe they belonged to Harold Stevens." Annie tossed the theory out there like a trial balloon.

"Nonsense!" Stella said, again. "Harold Stevens is no more a hero than I am. Why, when he came home from the war, he was angry and bitter. Changed. And not for the better, I'll tell you."

Annie caught her breath, excited. "What do you mean? What do you know about Harold?"

"I know a lot about Harold Stevens. Those were good days, before the war. Before I left Stony Point. Of course you know I was younger than Betsy, but she took me under her wing and treated me like a sister. I attended a lot of events with her in those days."

"What does that have to do with Harold?" Mary Beth asked.

"Betsy and Harold were high school sweethearts. I used to go with them sometimes to the movies. Betsy said I was her chaperone."

Annie and Alice exchanged knowing looks. Another confirmation about Betsy and her first love.

"Harold was wild about her. And she was just as crazy about him. Everyone thought they would marry. But something happened." Stella seemed subdued, her voice tinged with regret.

Annie shifted in her chair. Was she going to hear that her grandfather had stolen Harold's girl? A knot formed in her stomach. She hesitated, and then finally asked, "What about my grandpa?"

"Charlie? He didn't come into the picture until after the war. By then, Harold and Betsy had broken up."

Relief flooded Annie's heart. How could she have doubted her grandfather for one minute? His reputation as an honorable man was engraved in Stony Point history.

"So what happened?" Alice prompted Stella, who had apparently paused to live among her memories again.

"To Harold and Betsy?" Stella lifted her knitting again, her needles poised for purling.

"Yes!" The ladies replied in unison. They were in need-to-know territory now.

"That," Stella said, pausing for effect, "is a mystery still. Harold broke it off with Betsy even before he came home. Sent her a 'Dear Jane' letter. She was devastated, to put it mildly."

"But you don't know why?" Annie asked.

"My opinion? Thought himself a lady's man. Every girl in Stony Point was flirting with him before he left for the war. He did look fine in that uniform." Then Stella looked disgusted.

"And what happened to Gram?"

"The joy seemed to be gone out of Betsy's life. 'Gone to sea with Harold,' she'd say." Stella began to knit again. "I thought they'd get back together after the war. But it was impossible."

"Why?" She was glad that Gram had married Grandpa but still. . .she wanted the whole story.

"When Harold came home, he was different." Stella pursed her lips, disapproving, and knitted faster. "He was like a storm cloud waiting to break open with hurricane force. Drinking. Angry. Sullen. People just left him alone. I think that's what he wanted all along. I heard later that he married Caroline from Portland and spent most of his time out fishing. Then Charlie came to town and, well, you know the rest."

Annie sat back. She had learned much, but felt more confused than ever.

If Stella didn't know who owned the medals, who did? And what was the problem with Harold at the end of the war? Grandpa and Gram, the only ones who might have been able to answer her questions, were no longer here to ask.

The answers lay with the tight-lipped Harold Stevens.

And as Alice might say, good luck with that.

~ 23 ~

Once the rain let up, Annie and Alice headed outside to regroup under clearing skies. The streets glistened, reflecting the afternoon sun streaming through swollen clouds. Sea gulls, wings flapping gracefully, cried out as they coasted overhead.

"What shall we do now?" Alice asked, glancing up and down Main Street as if the next clue might walk out of a shop and introduce itself.

Annie thought a moment and then outlined her plan. "We'll start at the library. Let's get Grace Emory to do a search on Harold Stevens. We need to look under every stone if we hope to unearth this secret he has kept so long."

"Grace Emory. Good. What else?"

"After that, I want to talk to Ian Butler. If Harold was awarded the Medal of Honor, maybe the mayor can help. He was a Navy man, after all," Annie said.

"Yes, ma'am." Alice received her orders, laughing.

They trekked past the Cup and Saucer and crossed Oak Lane, sidestepping puddles, hurrying up under the pillared porch of the Stony Point Library. Annie pushed open the door and made her way into the Great Room, sla-loming between tables toward circulation. Alice followed close behind. The room was scattered with users, some tapping away on laptops, some in comfy chairs.

One look at Valerie Duffy stationed at the circulation desk told Annie that Grace must be at reference. Motioning to Alice, Annie aimed deeper into the building. Soon they waited in line behind an older woman receiving assistance with her genealogy search. Annie's impatience surged to the surface, frustrating her. She didn't want to resort to toe-tapping in front of anyone. And what was the big hurry, anyway? She sought a distraction.

"Have you seen Gram's cross-stitch in the rare book case?" Annie led the way through the reference collection until they stopped in front of the display. She sensed the awe Alice was feeling. She had felt it herself.

"Moving, isn't it? I remember Gram stitching this very piece one summer when I visited."

Alice was silent for a time. "I love how the beam from Butler's Lighthouse provides the way to safe harbor. The guiding light. Betsy really captures that message in this piece."

They gazed at the picture, each seeing different aspects of its beauty, until a voice behind them interrupted their reverie.

"I saw you two waiting in line." Grace seemed almost upbeat today, the sparkle in her eyes at least a tiny reflection of her signature diamond stud earrings. "Did you come to visit your gram's masterpiece?"

"I did. It's so nice that the public can see it anytime they like. That must have pleased Gram," Annie said, smiling at the thought.

"Absolutely. We talked about that very thing. Though

I always told Betsy I was going to steal that picture right out of the case. I have access to the key, you know."

Grace seemed to be joking. But Annie couldn't tell for sure.

"Enough about my life of crime. How may I help?"

Annie explained what they needed. "Anything you can find on Harold Stevens' military service."

"Pictures, facts, rumors, lies, whatever." Alice added her several cents.

"Ladies!" Grace actually laughed a little. "This sounds suspicious. But my job isn't to evaluate your motives. It's to investigate and inform. I'll let you know what I find."

Back outside and on their way to town hall, Annie said to Alice, "I didn't know Grace could be so much fun. The last time I was here, she seemed almost morose. What do you think happened?"

"You got me." Alice apparently had no insights.

They hiked across the lush lawns of the town square, the stars and stripes snapping a greeting. Annie stood a little straighter as they passed, her American pride pinging her heart. The area was empty, giving it an almost solemn air. Like a cemetery.

As the women climbed the steps to the imposing town hall entrance, Annie wondered if they should be wearing their casual clothes. No, the citizens of Stony Point looked on the inside of a person. Not the outside.

She breathed in the fresh salt air and opened the door wide.

"After you," Annie said to Alice, bowing a little. Both walked into the spacious foyer, Annie heading to the hall where Ian's office was located.

Alice wandered away, moving across the room and lingering there. "Annie, can you come over here for a minute? I think you'll be interested in this." Her voice was quiet, but compelling.

"Sure." Turning, Annie walked to where Alice stood staring at a large exhibit titled, "Stony Point Celebrates Local Artisans." Inside the glass case were various examples of art: a pen-and-ink drawing of the pier, a deep-sea adventure novel, a vintage quilt with blocks in a boat pattern, an exquisite necklace made of sea glass, smooth wood sculptures of marine life, and all manner of artistic output. Next to each sat a small card imprinted with the artist's name and the date the piece was produced. Some were antiques, some recent. Fascinated, Annie took in the rich sample of Stony Point creativity at a glance before her gaze was pulled to one piece in particular.

She caught her breath.

In one corner sat Gram's cross-stitch pillow. The piece Annie had donated to the auction. The superbly stitched harbor scene spoke to the crux of coastal Maine history. To her, the design tied together all the other examples of life by the sea. A grin spread across Annie's face, unbidden.

"Look at the card," Alice said, pointing.

Annie read the tiny text aloud. "Betsy Holden. Safe Harbor Cross-Stitch. From the private collection of Grace Emory."

She spun around to face Alice. "So that was it! Grace bought Gram's pillow. That's why she seemed so pleased. Doesn't it look wonderful on display here?"

Warmth rushed over Annie as she realized that this treasure had a home with someone who would appreciate and understand its true value. In truth, maybe the pillow had been a little lost among so many of Gram's other items at Grey Gables.

"Okay, let's go. I know parting is sweet sorrow and all that, but you can visit the pillow on our way out," Alice said, dragging Annie away from the exhibit.

Annie peered backward at the display until they rounded the corner and headed down the hallway. A short walk and they came to Mayor Butler's office.

Mrs. Nash, the secretary, seemed glad to see them. "Do you want to see the mayor? You're in luck. I believe he's available. Let me check just to be sure."

She jumped up from her chair, showing more athleticism than expected by the look of her silvered curls. Annie saw that the cyborg telephone attachment she'd noticed on the last visit still grew out of the secretary's ear.

When Mrs. Nash reappeared, she waved them into the mayor's office. He stood behind his desk, a massive oak arrangement of thick legs and deep drawers. He indicated that Annie and Alice should sit in a couple of the dark leather chairs placed nearby. Once they seemed comfortable, Ian sat in a matching office chair.

"Welcome, both of you. How goes the investigation?"

"We have so much to tell you!" Annie began to pour out all they had learned from Harold, Commander Bruce, and Stella. The mayor sat quietly, not interrupting as she spun her story.

"A Medal of Honor? I should have known about that,

Annie. Stony Point history is my passion." Ian's expression filled with regret. "How did that amazing fact slip by me?"

"Well, there is a little twist. Stella says it can't possibly be Harold's or we *would* know about it," Annie said.

"Isn't that what you are saying, Mayor?" Alice asked.

"Indeed it is," the mayor said. "But we have the facts we need to find out for sure. As Commander Bruce said, it's all right there on the Internet."

"I have asked Grace Emory to do a search." Annie leaned forward. "If anyone can learn the truth, she can. I bet we know something before the day is out!"

"If only we'd known we could have just used a computer to find out!" Alice said, exasperated. "That gives me a headache."

Ian chuckled. "Now you're being too hard on yourself, Alice. Until we knew that we were looking for a Medal of Honor recipient, we were just trolling for information, hoping facts would jump in the boat. It's a lucky break for us that we are talking about such a prestigious medal. A lesser one would have been even tougher to track."

"There's more," Annie said, adding the story of her grandmother's romance with Harold and their breakup. "No one seems to know why."

Annie went on, filling in with Harold's weird personality change after the war.

"We think we may know who the medals belong to, but even if I could return them to Harold, he wouldn't want them. Denies he ever earned them."

"Did he say that exactly? I thought you said he claimed he didn't deserve them," Alice said. "Technically, he didn't say he never earned them, right?"

Annie gasped. "My goodness, you're right! He said they weren't his. And that he didn't deserve them. Clever man. He fooled me."

The mayor sat back in his chair, thoughtful now. "If you don't mind, I'd like to do a little digging, apart from Grace's efforts. Call some of my contacts from the service. I'm as anxious to find out the truth about this as you are, Annie. Harold has been a lifelong citizen of Stony Point. If he is the recipient, I'd like to see him get the recognition he deserves."

"Good luck with that," Alice said.

"There's one more thing you might need in order to find out the whole truth, Ian," Annie said. "The story behind a Dorothy Divine. Harold said he got himself in trouble over this woman. But he wouldn't say more."

After making a few notes, Ian looked up. "Got it. You two have done well. I might have to put you on the payroll as researchers or something."

"There's something else," Alice said, looking pointedly at Annie, who didn't respond with more than a "Who, me?" expression.

"Really? I can't wait to hear this," Ian said, leaning back in his chair as if ready for a good story.

"Annie, I think you need to tell our mayor what you told me in the car. About the possible attempt on your life?" Alice said.

The mayor sat forward, concern crossing his face. "What's this all about?"

"Oh, that," Annie said, flatly. She didn't really want to

play the victim in front of Ian. He had already witnessed her introduction to car theft. What would he think if she suggested that some person had initiated what was probably just an act of nature? Did she really believe a person was behind it?

Okay, yes, she did. But maybe she was wrong. Still, knowing a good deal about Alice's tenacity told Annie she might as well spill her news now. She'd have to eventually, anyway. "Well, remember I told you I'd made a visit to see Harold?"

The mayor nodded, listening.

After Annie had filled in all the details for Ian, he took very little time to consider the matter. "Annie, it sounds like you have tread upon something here that has put you in real jeopardy. I think you should continue your search with the utmost care. Watch your back, so to speak."

"And your sides and your front, if you ask me," Alice said. "I'm going to stay close by Annie. You can be sure of that, Ian."

"As I said before, I'm going to dig deeper into this and try to speed it to a quick conclusion. The sooner we figure this out, the better. For everyone's sake," he said, looking back and forth at his visitors. The mayor's troubled gaze rested longest on Annie. "You. . .be careful. We wouldn't want anything to happen to Betsy's granddaughter. I consider your safety a trust for the town. So, please, take care."

The women rose to leave, Ian rising also. Offering thanks, they gathered their purses and walked to the office door.

Annie paused, almost afraid to ask a last question. "Did you find out if there were any other items stolen during the auction?"

"No, Annie. Yours was the only theft reported. I'm sorry."

She was sorry, too. Now Annie knew she was a target.

～ 24 ～

uesday morning, Annie arose earlier than usual. After another sleep-deprived night, she was exhausted and jittery at the same time. As soon as she had settled into her soft sheets, another creak or bump would sound. Each time, Annie jumped up, armed with no more than a crochet hook, and crept through the house. Of course, she found nothing and no one. But by 2:00 A.M., Boots had apparently tired of the interruptions and leaped off the bed, loping down-stairs to her corner on the sofa.

All the creepy noises aside, rest had eluded Annie, her brain battered with questions. Parts of the story were still missing. If Harold was a hero, why wouldn't he want his medals? Why did his and Grandpa's friendship dissolve? And did the answers have anything to do with the unsettling things that had happened to her lately?

One thing for sure, Annie was determined to solve this mystery, and soon. If only for a good night's rest.

"Hello? Annie?" Alice's cheery voice carried down the hall. "Anybody home?"

"In here," Annie said, too tired to get up and greet her guest.

Alice entered the kitchen. "Not to be a nagger, but your front door was open. I just walked right in."

She pulled a mug off of the exposed cupboard shelf, inspected it, and wiped it with a dish towel. "Dusty."

"The kitchen stays in its dusty mode. Waiting for Wally. . .and you, of course." Annie leaned her elbows on the table for support. "That's why I unlocked the door." She half-heartedly pushed a plate of Alice's pumpkin scones across the table.

"What's wrong with you?" asked Alice. "Did you just give blood? Run a mile? You look awful."

"Don't I wish. Just tired, bushed, drained, worn out. Pick one." Annie sipped her coffee.

Strange. The cup seemed much heavier than usual.

But then, it was a very strong coffee.

Alice filled her mug with steamy water from the kettle. "Bad night?" she asked, pulling out a chair and sitting opposite Annie.

"Very bad. We have to solve this mystery soon or I'll end up a live zombie."

"I don't think you can be a live zombie," Alice said. "Besides, that ashen look isn't good on you. Not with your peaches and cream complexion." She bit into a scone.

Annie attempted a smile. "Crazy lady."

A loud, insistent knock on the front door caused Annie to push herself away from the table with great effort. "Why doesn't Wally just come around back if he's uncomfortable coming in the front door? He does it when I'm gone." Her voice faded.

"I'll get it." Alice was off in a flash to stop the knock.

She returned with Ian Butler in tow. "It wasn't Wally, after all." She shrugged, as if she didn't want to let anyone in, but it was the mayor, for goodness' sake.

"Morning, Mr. Mayor." Annie took a deep breath, pasting on her happy face. "I'm surprised to see you, but you are most welcome to one of Alice's excellent scones. They're pumpkin." She indicated he should sit.

"Coffee, Ian?" Alice asked, a mug in one hand.

"Thanks, no. Can't stay. But I wanted to give you this information personally." He seemed excited as he opened a folder and drew out some printed pages, handing one to Annie. "Look at this."

She scanned the information, her brows arching in wonder. "My goodness! This is a Medal of Honor citation. For Harold Stevens." She passed the paper on to Alice. "Where did you find it?"

"Internet." Ian offered her another sheet. "That's not all."

"What's this?" Annie frowned as she read.

Ian sat down between the women. "Once I found Harold's citation, I made some calls. One of my contacts sent me this report." He handed her another page. "This is why Harold says he doesn't deserve the medals. He was court-martialed."

"What? Our Harold Stevens? Why?" Annie asked.

"Manslaughter. He killed a man. And was incarcerated in the brig. After the court-martial, the military ordered him stripped of all medals and honors."

"No wonder he didn't want to talk about it," Alice said, shaking her head sadly.

"I don't understand." Annie said. "How could the medals in the attic be Harold's if he was already stripped of them?"

"Most likely, the tribunal didn't demand Harold return the medals. They simply removed his right to wear them and all the benefits the honors bestow. The Medal of Honor is our highest military decoration, usually presented by the President. Being stripped of your medals is a huge fall from grace."

"Wow." Alice's expression was one of wonder. "But he could have worn them anyway, right? Because he still had them. Who would know?"

"No serviceman of honor would ever do that. The few that chanced it have paid a stiff penalty. Very special privileges are also attached to this honor, like a pension or having one's children eligible to attend military academies."

Annie looked thoughtful. "I just can't believe Harold is a killer. Not after being so honorable and brave. How did it happen?"

Mayor Butler pointed to the report. "A bar fight. Looks like it was accidental, but the testimonies conflicted a good deal. If it had been murder, Harold would never have been released at the end of the war."

"Maybe he covered for someone else. What was his defense?" Annie asked. "Or maybe those other testimonies conflicted with his account, and that's why he was found guilty."

"According to this report, Harold refused to testify in his own defense. With the damning evidence presented, the outcome was obvious." Ian put the report back in the folder. "One is left wondering if he simply had no defense."

"Or could there be another reason for his silence? What about Dorothy Divine?" Annie asked. She didn't want that lonely old man to be condemned forever. Not by the military, not by himself. There had to be more to the story.

Ian seemed to sympathize with her unspoken longing. "I searched yesterday afternoon. Finally I obtained her last address through my military contacts. Unfortunately she's deceased. But I contacted her daughter, Mrs. Bonnie Gleeson. I explained about Harold. Bonnie said she has information we need. I'm awaiting a fax from her later this morning."

"That's incredible!" Annie's excitement acted like adrenalin. "What now?"

"We meet with Harold. Maybe have his son and grandson there, too. He may need their support. Once we tell him what we know, he may fill in the details for us. We'll finally get this solved!"

"Let's go!" Annie said, bursting from her chair like a thoroughbred through a starting gate. "I could call Kate. Maybe she could set something up this morning."

Ian stood. "Let me do the honors. I have a feeling a call from the mayor's office might have a better response than even Kate Stevens could elicit."

"What about me?" Alice rose, ready for action.

"Would you mind waiting for Wally? I have some things for him to do that need a woman's detailed explanation. There's a list," Annie said. "Then you could pop over to the Hook and Needle Club meeting and bring the ladies up to speed."

"But I'll miss all the fun! After helping you out, Annie? Don't I deserve to be there?" Alice said in a peevish voice.

"Actually, Alice, that's a good idea." The mayor spoke kindly. "But this is Harold's life we are talking about. It's a sensitive issue. He doesn't know you. The fewer folks who witness his statement, the better."

Defeated by common sense, Alice nodded. "I guess."

Ian turned to Annie. "Meet me at Ocean View Assisted Living at eleven. We'll see what happens from there." They walked down the hall, discussing the plan. Passing the living room, Annie stopped to scoop up a cardboard box containing the new afghan, ready to post to Texas.

"I want to put this in the mail while I'm in town," she told the mayor in explanation.

A quick wave to Alice, and Annie was out the door.

～ 25 ～

Annie sat in the open reception area of the assisted-living facility. She crossed and uncrossed her legs at the ankles, nervous but excited, too. What if they could somehow give Harold Stevens a different ending to his story?

The double doors opened and Mayor Butler herded Robert and Harry Stevens, Harold's son and grandson, into the room. "Come on in, gentlemen. I appreciate your prompt arrival. We'll try not to keep you long."

They both grunted their answers, looks of annoyance on their faces at this unexpected interference in their day's work.

"What's she doing here?" Harry asked, his bad attitude on full display.

"My apologies. I don't believe you've met Mrs. Annie Dawson." Ian made the introductions. "Mrs. Dawson is the granddaughter of Dr. Charlie and Betsy Holden. You remember them, right?"

More grunts in the affirmative.

"Good. Mrs. Dawson is joining us today as we visit Harold. We'd like to talk to him, and we need you there for his support." Mayor Butler put his hand out. "Lead the way."

Robert and Harry headed into the activity room with Annie and Ian close behind. Covered in the ratty afghan again, Harold sat alone, staring out at his beloved sea. When he turned and saw his son and grandson approach, his expression changed from lost to loving in a heartbeat.

"Robert! And Harry, too? What a surprise. Thanks for coming, guys."

Annie watched the men hug one another, noting the affection across generations. Obviously Harold was esteemed by his family. She couldn't accept that he was a killer, no matter what the report said.

Ian stepped forward. "Mr. Stevens, I hope you don't mind the interruption. Mrs. Dawson and I have come, too. We wanted to talk to you, with your boys present. Would that be all right?" Ian clamped a friendly hand on the senior's shoulder.

"Sure, sure," Harold said, apparently unaware that his world was about to change. "Good to see you, Mayor. Mrs. Dawson."

"Just call me Annie." She smiled at him, hoping for a happy ending. "Betsy's granddaughter, remember?"

"Right. . .Annie. You stopped by the other day." He grinned, showing a hint of the boyish charm that must have won over Annie's grandmother.

Harold was winning her over, too.

"Let's sit in a circle so we can keep our voices down." Ian pulled some chairs near, and soon they were all seated close to Harold. Robert threw a protective arm around his father. Harry leaned back, arrogant.

Annie started the conversation. "Do you remember

when we spoke last week? I asked if you had been awarded any medals. You said you didn't deserve any."

Harold nodded, his eyes clouding. "I remember."

"But we have learned that during the war, you were awarded not only a Purple Heart, but the Medal of Honor, as well."

Harry jumped up. "You don't know what you're talking about! Leave him alone!" He moved closer to his grandfather.

Robert stared at his father, worry in his eyes.

The old man slumped in his chair, hanging his head. "So it will all come out?"

Harry stared at Annie, almost hissing when he spoke. "You. . .you. . .busybody! What right do you have poking your nose into our affairs? No right at all! My grandfather has a right to his privacy. He never hurt you. He never hurt anybody."

"That's not completely true, Harry, and you know it," Annie said.

Robert broke his silence. "Back off, Harry. Now too many people know about Dad's past. Give it up."

"No!" Harry said through clenched teeth, shaking his fist at Annie. "*You* back off! This is none of your business. I won't let you hurt Pops. He's the best man I know."

Ian stepped forward and clasped Harry's arm, forcing his hand back down and then releasing it. "We can discuss this without anger. This lady doesn't deserve your disdain. She has earned my respect by seeking the truth, no matter where it led her."

"Respect? Bah!" Harry almost spit out the words. "I've

got no respect for busybodies who can't recognize a good man when they see one."

"I do see one. Right here," Annie pointed to Harold. "What we are trying to do is restore the honor that belongs to his good name, so it can be recognized."

Harry shook his head. "I don't believe you."

"I find it hard to believe, as well," Robert said, still seated next to his father, his arm encircling the veteran. "We've been protecting my dad for so long. Protecting ourselves, too, from any fallout from the exposure." He pulled back, ran his fingers through thick black hair, and looked up at Annie. "How can it be okay to talk about it now? Today? When it wasn't okay yesterday?"

"Harold, does your family know the whole story?" Annie asked gently.

"The boys know. They've had to bear the shame of—" Harold couldn't seem to finish his thought.

"We have some information that might change the way you see it," Annie said with more authority than she had a right to convey. "But we have questions, too. May we ask them so we can establish the truth and restore your honor?"

"You can't rewrite history," he said dully. He turned toward his grandson. "Harry, please sit down. You've protected me. But I don't need protection from Mayor Butler or from Betsy Holden's granddaughter."

He waved to a chair and Harry sat, his mouth drawn in a thin line.

After everyone was again seated, Annie asked, "Mr. Stevens, can you just tell us your story, in your own words?"

Harold nodded and cleared his throat.

"Do you need some water, Pops? Are you comfortable?" Harry asked, leaning toward his grandfather.

"It's a little chilly in here," Harold said, shivering.

Harry reached over and pulled up the worn afghan, tucking it around the senior Stevens' legs. "This old thing lets in more cold than it keeps out. I'm going to have to learn to crochet myself and make you a new one."

Harold chuckled a little, in spite of the situation. "It would be hard to replace this old blanket. Handmade by your grandmother, Harry."

"I know." Harry sat back down, his eyes on Harold, apparently watching for signs of discomfort.

Annie, touched by the demonstration, choked up and was unable to speak for a moment. Finally she recovered. "Go ahead, Mr. Stevens. Anytime you are ready."

"I've lived with this for so long," he whispered. "Covering it up has cost me. Friends couldn't get too close. I didn't join any post-military activities. And it hurt my boys, here. Made you afraid for me. Made you feel ashamed, too, though you had no reason to be. For that, I'm sorry." He shook his head.

"I started with a bad attitude. And it was the war! After I got the medals, I got cocky. I was young, a hero. . . full of myself."

"What I don't understand," Annie said, interrupting, "is why notice of your Medal of Honor never made it to Stony Point. I mean, this is a huge honor. Wouldn't your family be contacted? Wouldn't there be press releases?"

Harold raised his eyebrows. "That was my question,

too. At first. I wrote my mom that she'd be getting good news soon. I thought the Navy would make the announcement. I wanted that ring of authority that comes with a message from the government. Not me. But it was the war."

"It never came?" Ian asked.

"It never did," Harold said. "It was wartime, and my awards were given at sea. I'd been wounded in battle, and it was some time before I was ready to receive them. After the ceremony on the ship, I was shipped stateside for more treatment."

"Did you convalesce on board the USS *Beneficent*?" Annie asked, excited. "Is that where you met Charles Holden? My grandpa?"

"Yes. I recovered from my most severe wounds aboard his hospital ship. He used to listen as I talked about Stony Point. Oh, how I wanted to get home! I told him about Betsy, though I'd broken off our relationship by then." Harold smiled, gazing out to sea. "That's where Charlie and I became friends. He stuck by me through everything."

"You were saying that it was wartime when you received your medals." Ian brought the conversation back on topic. "Please continue."

"Right." Harold pulled the shabby afghan up around his chest and gave a couple of shallow coughs, covering his mouth with a calloused hand. He cleared his throat again.

In an instant, Harry was back on his feet, accusing. "Don't you see he can't handle all this? Can't you just leave him alone?"

~ 26 ~

*H*arold spoke up then. "I'm fine now, Harry. Where was I?"

"It was wartime . . ." Ian helped him along.

"Yes, it was wartime, and the action was sufficient that radio silence was imposed at various times. Even during the ceremony at sea. Normal press releases were always timed to the actual ceremony. But I found out later that the office that would release the information never got word because of the prolonged radio silence.

"I didn't know about the omission for a time. I thought it strange that my mother never congratulated me. Nor did anyone else. Except Charlie and my crewmates."

Harold chuckled. "There was another reason that no one heard about it. Talk about government bureaucracy! Charlie had gone stateside not long after I was awarded the medals. He had a friend who was an assistant in an office in Washington, where those kinds of press releases were sent out. Charlie asked him to check into it.

"Later he said that they found the releases in a desk drawer in D.C. The name of my town had been mis-spelled. And they couldn't figure out which town to send it to; there were three towns it could have been. So the press release never got sent. And that's a good thing, too, because of the trouble I got into."

"What do you mean?" Annie asked.

"I was glad no one knew. There was no mention of any medals, especially the Medal of Honor, by anyone at home. It was like it never happened. Almost as if the oversight was providential. Thank you, Uncle Sam."

"Can you tell us what trouble you got into?" Ian asked.

Harry let out an angry grunt and crossed his arms, looking away.

"It was awful." Harold studied his hands, clasping and unclasping them several times before he spoke. "It was soon after I was awarded the medals. I was pretty full of myself. I had broken up with Betsy so I could romance the girls—many girls. Maybe I thought that was a point of honor; I wouldn't fool around while she still thought we were a couple. But it's not much to hang my cap on."

He took a deep breath. "I drank a lot. Too much. More, whenever I got liberty. One night, I got into a fight, in a bar, defending a woman. Only it turned out badly. And a man ended up dead—by my hand."

Harold hesitated, tearing up, the pain in his eyes evident. "I didn't mean it. I swear I never meant to kill him."

Robert reached around his father's shoulder again, resting his arm in acceptance. "Of course not, Dad. Anyone who knows you believes that."

"I was court-martialed and found guilty of manslaughter."

The mayor leaned toward Harold. "Why didn't you defend yourself, sir?"

"Because," Harold said, "I couldn't. I was drunk at

the time and couldn't remember anything. And there were witnesses who said I was guilty. So how could that be defended?"

"Apparently a lot of the witnesses were also drunk. You might have been exonerated if all the evidence had been presented," Ian said.

"I only remember this man bullying the woman who had taken care of me in the hospital. When he slapped her, I hit him. Knocked him across the room. Banged his head against the bar."

Harold sighed deeply. "I did it. No one else. They stripped me of my medals and revoked my pay. I spent the remainder of my tour of duty in the brig. After the war, I was sent packing with a dishonorable discharge."

"Dad, you made a mistake is all." Robert's voice wavered as he patted the old man on the back. "We've always known about the court-martial, and we love you anyway."

"Yeah," said Harry, "we've always known. I had that secret thing hanging over my head until I was eighteen. 'When you turn eighteen, Harry, you'll learn the family secret.' I thought it would be some wonderful thing to carry through life," Harry's anger rose as he turned on his grandfather. "Why didn't you just take it to the grave, Pops? You think I want to have that talk with Vanessa when she turns eighteen?"

Harold shook his head. "I'm so very sorry, Harry. I thought it was the right thing to do. I hoped that Robert and you would steer clear of trouble if you knew how I had ruined my life."

Harry's shoulders sagged as if he was surrendering his anger to his love for his grandfather. "Forget what I said, Pops. I didn't mean it."

"I know you didn't, Harry." Harold's big hands trembled. "I never meant for you boys to live with my shame."

"We're doing okay, Dad," Robert said. "We have a great life. I've been working my program for what? Twelve years? Put my marriage back together, keeping the business afloat, doing the Stevens name proud. Harry's doing okay, too, aren't you, son?"

Eyes downcast, Harry agreed with a nod of his head.

"What happened to the medals?" Annie asked. Maybe she would finally understand how they came to be in Gram's attic.

"When I came home, I left the medals behind. I couldn't wear them or claim them. Didn't deserve them. Especially not a Medal of Honor. Just left them in my locker. Charlie brought them to me later, not long after the war ended."

"Then how did he end up keeping your medals? I can't figure it out," Annie said. "Why would he bring you medals you couldn't wear, in the first place?"

Harold peered into the distance, retrieving the memory like nets full of fish. "I have so many regrets. Especially the way I treated Charlie. He was a good friend. He knew the full story about the man who was killed, and he never condemned me. He said he thought that by returning the medals, I'd be reminded of the good I had done, the lives that were saved and my part in it.

"When he arrived in Stony Point, I was on a fishing

trip. Charlie had to hang around town for three days, waiting. He'd heard about Betsy when I was on the *Beneficent,* and he looked her up. Not for any other reason than to talk about me, find out how I was doing. Charlie learned then that no one was aware of my war service, the good or the bad. So he kept what he knew to himself. He was a true friend, that Charlie.

"He and Betsy seemed to get on well. He met some of Betsy's friends, too, including Stella. Anyway, once I got back from fishing, I heard Charlie was in town and looking for me. I wasn't too anxious to see him, as you might imagine, but we met down at South Beach. Where no one else could hear our conversation.

"When he gave me back the medals, I was angry. Probably at myself, mostly. I threw those medals far out to sea. Didn't want to see them. Didn't want to be reminded of them. Didn't want anyone to know what had happened. I guess I didn't throw them far enough. Charlie always said I was lousy at throwing." A grin crept across his lips.

"My grandfather must have found them later on the beach. And he kept them for you all these years. In fact, he built a case for them and carved patriotic symbols on it." Annie said. "It's really quite beautiful."

"That was Charlie for you."

"Pops, why haven't you ever told us these details? We don't even know what you did to win a Medal of Honor. When we've asked, you wouldn't talk about it. All we've been told is about your faults and your disgrace."

"I don't deserve any accolades," Harold said, clamping his mouth closed.

"That's not true, sir," Ian said. "And your son and grandson deserve to know about your bravery. What happened in that bar does not negate your courage under fire, medals or no medals." Mayor Butler opened his folder and took out a paper. "This is a copy of the citation you received for your Medal of Honor. May I read it?"

In a new act of courage, Harold indicated his approval with a nod. Robert and Harry waited, silent.

"I'll skip the legalese and read the actual act of valor concerning Harold Robert Stevens:

For extraordinary heroism and conspicuous gallantry in action above and beyond the call of duty as Boat-swain's Mate Third Class, engaged in a rescue effort during combat against enemy Japanese aerial forces near Lunga Point at Guadalcanal, on 10 August 1942. After watching his ship's response to the distress call of a nearby supply ship result in the loss of 2 lifeboats carrying 6 crewmembers by enemy aerial gunfire, Boatswain's Mate Third Class Harold Stevens low-ered a third lifeboat and initiated yet another rescue attempt. Under constant strafing by enemy machine guns from the air, with a clear and present danger and at great risk to his life, Boatswain's Mate Third Class Harold Stevens daringly rowed his craft toward his crewmates. As he closed the distance to the first man in the water, the strafing hit nearby wood hull debris and a shard pierced Boatswain's Mate Third Class Harold Stevens' side. Though severely wounded and amid fierce enemy fire, he rowed onward, sin-gle-handedly effecting the rescue of his shipmates. Together they rescued another 27 men from the water,

*trapped by strafing from enemy forces. His excep-
tionally heroic act in the face of extremely perilous
combat conditions enabled him and his courageous
comrades to undoubtedly save the lives of many who
otherwise would have perished and reflects the highest credit upon Boatswain's Mate Third Class Harold
Stevens and the U.S. Naval Service.*

The mayor stopped reading then, allowing the truth of
Harold's heroism to sink into the hearts of his family. The
old man stared out to sea, perhaps remembering. Robert's
eyes teared up, and he hugged his father. "I'm so proud of
you, Dad."

Harry held his head in his hands. Annie wasn't sure
if he was overcome with emotion at learning of his grandfather's bravery or just weary that it had taken so long for
it to be revealed.

"Too bad I messed up," Harold said with regret. "Once,
I had it all. But, as the boys know, I did stop drinking." He
smiled at the boys.

"You gave all you had to save the lives of your men."
Annie wanted him to hold onto this source of pride again.
He had shown incredible courage back then. And she was
sure he'd been brave many times since. Grandpa Holden
used to say that honor cannot be lost when it is at the core
of one's character.

Just then, the receptionist tapped Ian on the shoulder.
"Sorry to interrupt, Mr. Mayor. But there is someone here
to see you. Can you follow me?"

Without any explanation, the mayor left the room.

～ 27 ～

Returning quickly, Ian examined another sheet of paper as he stood among them. "My secretary just dropped off this fax. It contains new information that may change the way you look at your past, Mr. Stevens." Annie looked over at Harold, who wore a doubtful expression. "You mentioned to Mrs. Dawson a woman named Dorothy Divine."

Harold nodded his assent. "That's right. She was the nurse on base when I was flown stateside after being wounded. I was interested in her, but rumor had it she was married. Still, a guy can enjoy the scenery." His smile broadened.

"No argument from me, sir," Ian said. "According to this report, she was the person you were defending that night in the bar."

"That's right. That brute she was with was just that. An animal. You know what I mean."

"I do." The mayor nodded. "What *you* don't know is the rest of the story. Ms. Divine was indeed married to a very brutal man. According to this, he used to beat her often. She was afraid to escape from him, because he swore he'd always find her and nobody else could ever have her. 'Not that anyone would want her,' in his words."

"She took it. She was afraid. Poor woman," said Harold solemnly.

"I'm sorry to tell you that Dorothy Divine passed away two years ago. But I'd like to read a portion of this letter I received from her daughter, Bonnie Gleeson."

When Mr. Stevens stopped my biological father from dragging Mother out of the bar that night, she learned something—that she had value after all. Mother told me that though both men were intoxicated, the true nature of each was apparent. One was a devil, and the other, a hero. Harold Stevens saved my mother's life. He changed her life from that day forward. His act of chivalry gave her back her life that had been stolen by an evil man.

Harold Stevens saved my life, too. No one could have known that Mother was pregnant with me at that time. Even she didn't know. But in her words, Harold Stevens was her hero. She never forgot nor ceased to be grateful for his sacrifice. . .to her last breath.

"So you see, sir, you acted in a heroic fashion, even when you were drunk." Ian grinned. "To my mind, there are extenuating circumstances to this case. In fact, I'm prepared to assist you in an appeal of your conviction and the wrongful dishonorable discharge."

Harold's mouth dropped open in surprise. "You are? You'd do that, Mayor?"

"It would be a privilege." Ian held up an official-looking form. "I already have the Application for Correction of Military Records and will do all in my power to have this injustice reversed and all honors restored."

Robert slapped his father on the back. "Dad, that's amazing."

"Hear, hear!" Annie said, raising an imaginary glass.

Harold blinked rapidly. "I've lived with this shame for so long. How can I thank you both?"

Ian and Annie exchanged satisfied smiles.

"And my dad can get the medals he earned," Robert said, pride in his voice.

Annie sighed. How best to break the news about the missing medals? "Well, not exactly. I wish I could give them to you now, Mr. Stevens, but I lost them."

"Actually, they were stolen from Annie's car, along with a couple of old photos and a military file of Charlie's," Ian said. "The photos are probably gone for good, but I'm sure we can get the medals replaced once the appeal goes through. And copies of Charlie's separation papers, too," the mayor said to Annie.

"No need for that." Harry spoke for the first time and then stood. He exited the room, without a farewell.

Annie wondered at all this coming and going from their little session. Who would leave next? She was about to ask how Harold met his wife when Harry returned, carrying a large paper bag. He thrust it at her.

"I don't know any other way to do this," Harry said, barely making eye contact. "I took these from your car when I saw it parked in the church lot on Friday morning."

"You what?" Annie caught her breath and opened the bag. She saw the medals resting inside their case and the envelope which, she presumed, contained the old photos. Against the side of the bag, Grandpa's file stood at attention. A wave of anger washed over her, and her muscles tensed. She wanted to lash out or demand an explanation.

Yet somehow she couldn't collect her thoughts. She stared at Harry, speechless.

"Harry?" Confusion covered Harold's face. "Is that true? Did you steal from this young lady? Why would you do that?"

Shrugging, Harry began to explain, giving Annie an intense glare. "When Kate told me you all were poking around, asking questions about Pops, I thought you might discover his secret. I panicked. I just kept thinking, 'God forbid that it gets out because of a bunch of bored busybodies.' "

Annie bristled. It might be one thing for him to call her a busybody, but the entire Hook and Needle Club? That was going too far. And who said they were bored, anyway?

"Totally uncalled for, Harry," Ian said. "You owe Annie an apology."

"Stop it, son," Robert said, walking over to where Harry stood and placed a hand on his shoulder. "Take responsibility for your actions. You don't see your grandfather blaming a bunch of drunks for making him end up in prison, do you?"

"No. Guess not." Harry glanced up at Annie, like a petulant child. "Sorry."

Annie decided that was a sorry excuse for an apology. But, taking the high road, she said, "All right. I'll accept your apology for calling me and my friends busybodies. But I haven't heard anything remotely like an apology for stealing those medals or the rest of the stuff."

Harry pulled away from his father's touch, as if

Robert's hand on his shoulder burned. "They weren't your medals. They belonged to my grandfather! Why should I apologize for taking things that belonged to him?" Harry's stubborn behavior made Annie wonder how Kate put up with him as long as she had.

"Haven't you been listening, Harry?" Robert asked. "We're going to work to get your grandfather cleared, his medals restored. You are a descendant of a United States hero. You try to act like one."

"It's like you are still out leading the cavalry, and the war is over," the mayor said. "Truce, Harry. Back off. Quit protecting your grandfather. He doesn't need it anymore."

Then Harold's stern voice rang out. "Harry! I don't like to see this side of you. Do the right thing, now." His command had an immediate effect on his grandson.

Harry put his hands up in surrender. "Okay, Pops. You're right. And I apologize, Mrs. Dawson. I over-reacted that night. Maybe because I'd had a couple of drinks before I got to dinner. Clouded my thinking. A little fortification before meeting Kate."

Annie wondered how much fortification Harry had taken before meeting with the mayor this morning.

"What did Kate say that disturbed you so much?" Annie asked, trying to coax the truth from Harry. She might as well get the full story before she never spoke to him again.

"What didn't she say? Kate drives me nuts. Sometimes in a good way, sometimes bad. That night, she went on and on about you: how you crochet, how you dress, what you drive. . .she thinks you can do no wrong. After she talked about your World War II find, and Vanessa added that you were really good at solving mysteries, I thought that Pops' secret would get out. What could you have that might incriminate him? When I saw your car in the church lot. Unlocked, too," Harry said. "There in the back seat was some suspicious stuff. So I took it.

"Once I had it, I wasn't sure what to do with it. I couldn't give it to Pops. That would make a whole new problem. It was enough for me that you didn't have them, I guess." Harry blew out a deep breath. "It was wrong. I'm sorry."

So there it was, hanging out in space. Her apology. But Annie found herself not so inclined to accept. A stubborn streak was running right through her good judgment. She fell silent. All those days of worry and self-reprisal? When they were safe in Harry's keeping? She clutched the bag tighter, her fingernails digging into the paper.

On the other hand, she was relieved to get the medals back, along with the photos and Grandpa's file. If she didn't accept Harry's apology, did that mean more drama with Kate?

"Look, I've let everybody down. I know that." Harry gave a guilty glance toward his father and then the mayor, before returning his attention to Annie. "All I wanted was to make sure nobody hurt Pops." He took a few steps toward Harold and sat next to him, covering the old man's hand with his own.

Angry as she was, even Annie defrosted at the sight.

"Well, I guess because everything's back now, maybe we can just move on from here," Annie said, her best attempt at forgiveness, for now.

"Thanks, Mrs. Dawson. But—there's more."

~ 28 ~

*H*arry looked nervous. "The rock slide. Here at Ocean View. You. . .on the path to the landing. I started it."

Annie inhaled sharply. "What?"

"I'm so sorry, Mrs. Dawson. When I got that call from Tiffany at Seaside Hills, I knew you were serious about talking to Pops. I just meant it as a warning. To leave him alone. I never thought you might get hurt. I just wasn't thinking straight."

He massaged his brow, as if to ward off a thunderous headache. "It was wrong. I'm ashamed of myself."

Stunned at this new revelation, again Annie couldn't speak. This man, Kate's former husband, could have killed her. If she had missed grasping that wet rail when she stumbled. Well, she couldn't think about it. The outcome could have been disastrous.

"Harry, this is very serious. It's much more than petty theft." Ian shook a clenched fist. "Annie? Do you want to press charges? How shall we proceed?"

All eyes were on her, waiting for a decision. Annie could choose to send Harry straight to jail. No one would disagree. He confessed. And a part of Annie wanted to see him pay for the pain he'd put her through. Mental anguish, if not more. But then she thought of Kate, who still loved this terribly imperfect man. Weren't we all imperfect? She gazed at the three men: grandfather, son, and grandson. The love between them was so evident.

Annie hesitated only a moment more. "The agony ends now, Harry. I won't hold any of this against you today, or ever. In fact, I think Charlie Holden would have liked for me to pass off this mission to you."

She held the case out to Harry until he clasped it with both hands. He stared through the glass, apparently seeing for the first time the medals and the merit of the man who earned them.

"Thank you, Mrs. Dawson," Harry said, looking up, his eyes shining bright. "I will try hard to live up to my heritage."

In that moment, Annie could see the man that Kate saw. She smiled. "Call me Annie."

"Okay. . .Annie." He nodded and turned to Harold. "I'm proud to return these to you, Pops," Harry said, placing the case in his grandfather's lap with a kind of reverence. "You always were my hero."

The mayor snapped an official Navy salute to Harold. "A Medal of Honor winner is always saluted before anyone else in the room."

Harold saluted back, his eyes brimming with tears. And pride.

Mission accomplished.

"Now," Harold said, chuckling, as if to break the tension, "if someone could just do something about this old blanket." He indicated the tattered afghan, long past its best days.

Annie pictured a completed, crocheted afghan in colors of brick red, purple haze, sunshine gold, and chocolate. Only this morning, she had thought it bound for Texas. But now she wondered if an afghan made by the granddaughter of Harold's first love could offer comfort for the next season of his life.

The answer lay right outside, in the trunk of her car.

Excusing herself, Annie was the next person to leave the room.